Enid Blyton

BILLY-BOB TALES

First published 1938
Reprinted 1993

by Methuen & Co Ltd
This edition published 1991
by Dean, an imprint of
The Hamlyn Publishing Group
in association with Methuen Children's Books
an imprint of Octopus Publishing Group
Michelin House, 81 Fulham Road, London SW3 6RB

Copyright © Enid Blyton 1938

ISBN 0 416 17492 2

Printed in Italy

Enid Blyton's
BILLY-BOB
TALES

DEAN
IN ASSOCIATION WITH
METHUEN CHILDREN'S BOOKS

CONTENTS

Billy-Bob and Belinda go Shopping

ONCE UPON A TIME there was a little boy called William Robert, but everyone called him Billy-Bob for short. He was a happy little boy, with twinkling eyes, curly red hair, and a nose that turned up instead of down.

Billy-Bob had a sister smaller than himself. She was called Belinda, and she was rather fat. Her hair was yellow, not red, and she liked to do everything exactly like Billy-Bob.

Billy-Bob also had a dog called Wags. As soon as anyone saw Wags they couldn't help thinking what a good name he had – for he wagged his tail so hard that his body wagged too. Wags was what Daddy called a half-and-half dog – half good and half naughty – but Billy-Bob loved every bit of him from his cold wet nose to the last hair in his tail. He was Billy-Bob's own dog – not even Belinda shared him.

Billy-Bob, Belinda and Wags lived with their mother and father in a little house called Redroofs. It had white walls and a nice red roof, and the garden grew trees, flowers, vegetables and grass. It grew weeds as well, and sometimes, when the weeds were buttercups or dandelions, Billy-Bob thought they were just as pretty as the flowers.

Now one day Mother said a surprising thing. She said, 'Billy-Bob, I find I haven't enough butter, and I need some soap too. Would you like to go shopping for me, and get them?'

Now Billy-Bob had never in his life been to the village by himself before. This was a great treat! He stared at his mother in delight.

'I think you are old enough to be trusted now,' said Mother. 'There is only one road to cross, and I know you will look both ways before you run to the other side!'

'I want to go too,' said Belinda. Billy-Bob knew Belinda was going to say that. She always did.

'You are too little,' said Mother.

Belinda screwed up her eyes and opened her mouth very wide. Billy-Bob knew what was going to happen, so he spoke very quickly.

'Let Belinda come too, Mother. I'll look after her, really I will.'

Belinda thought she wouldn't howl before she had heard what Mother said, so she opened her eyes again and shut her mouth. She looked at Mother.

'Very well,' said Mother. 'Take hold of Belinda's hand and don't let it go till you get to the shops. Belinda, you are to be good. Don't take Wags, because you can't manage Belinda, the basket and Wags too.'

'I don't like Wags when he's on a lead,' said Billy-Bob. 'He winds himself round me so. Oh, Mother! I'm so excited to go shopping by myself! Are you going to give me some money in a purse too?'

'Yes,' said Mother. 'Here it is. There are five shillings in the purse in two half-crowns. You will have some change to bring back. Put on your coats and hats and run along quickly.'

'Here's your hat, Belinda, and here's your coat!' said Billy-Bob, in excitement. 'Don't be too long. Oh, you've got your hat back-to-front, Belinda. Don't you know which is which yet?'

At last they both had on their hats and coats. Belinda buttoned her coat all wrong, but Billy-Bob was too much in a hurry to notice that. He took up the basket, popped Mother's purse in the bottom, caught hold of Belinda's hand and went to kiss Mother goodbye.

He did feel important as he went down the

lane. He was sure that none of the other children he met were shopping for their mothers. Belinda trotted along beside him, puffing with excitement, holding his hand so tightly that it quite hurt Billy-Bob's fingers.

Soon they met Mister Clatter, the milkman, wheeling his noisy cart of bottles and cans.

'Good morning!' called Billy-Bob. 'I'm going shopping for my mother!'

'Goodness gracious!' said the milkman. 'Fancy you being big enough!'

Billy-Bob felt bigger still. He walked on, holding Belinda's hand, and met Sally, the balloon woman, carrying her big bundle of balloons to sell.

'I'm going shopping for my mother!' he called to her.

'Isn't she lucky to have a great boy like you!' said Sally, and Billy-Bob put his head up and felt a great boy indeed.

Suddenly something cold touched his legs. He looked down. It was Wags' wet nose!

'Oh, Wags!' he cried. 'Naughty dog! Go home! Mother said you weren't to come!'

'Wuff-wuff!' barked Wags and jumped round and round Billy-Bob and Belinda, getting between their legs every now and then.

'He'll have to go with us now, Belinda,' said Billy-Bob. 'We won't speak to him at all. He is a naughty dog.'

So on the two went, and Wags trotted behind, his tail wagging hard – but not a word did Billy-Bob and Belinda speak to him. They all crossed the road safely and went to the dairy for the butter. Billy-Bob felt very proud when he paid for it and took the change.

He put the butter into the basket and went to the grocer's. Mrs Spice gave them a packet of soap, and their change. Billy-Bob put it carefully into the purse, and then put the soap and the purse into the basket.

'It's a great day for you, shopping by yourselves,' said Mrs Spice, beaming at them. 'Would you like to choose one of my biscuits for yourselves? Come over here and choose.'

Billy-Bob put down the basket and he and Belinda went to choose a sugar biscuit each. They thanked Mrs Spice politely, and then danced out of the shop, most excited to think they had a biscuit each.

And then, oh dear! They hadn't gone very far when they remembered the basket – and Wags! They had left both behind in their excitement! How dreadful!

They ran back to the shop – but there was no basket there, and no Wags either. Mrs Spice didn't know anything about them.

Billy-Bob went red with shame. How *could* he do such a thing the very first time he had been trusted alone? He wasn't such a great boy after all. He was a very little boy.

'Come along home,' he said to Belinda. 'We must tell Mother.'

Belinda cried all the way – but Billy-Bob didn't. He was too big to cry in the street – but he wished he was as little as Belinda, so that he could!

'We've lost the shopping – and the change – and Wags too,' he kept saying to himself.

And then – just as they turned the corner down their lane, what *do* you think they saw? Guess!

They saw Wags – and in his mouth he carried the basket of shopping! He had noticed that they had left it behind, and had picked it up and run off another way home. Now he was waiting for them in the lane, his tail wagging so fast that it looked like the propeller of an aeroplane!

'Wags! Wags! Dear old Wags!' shouted Billy-Bob in joy. 'Is the soap there – and the butter – and the purse with the change in?'

'Wuff-wuff!' said Wags, as Billy-Bob took the

basket from him. Everything was there. Belinda dried her tears and laughed. Billy-Bob went down on his knees and hugged clever Wags.

'You're not a naughty dog, you're a very good one!' he cried.

Then off they ran to tell Mother all about it. 'It was a most exciting shopping, Mother,' said Billy-Bob. 'Can Wags have a sugar biscuit?'

'Wuff!' said Wags, and nearly wagged his tail off.

Billy-Bob Has a Surprise

BILLY-BOB AND BELINDA knew all the birds in their garden. Outside their dining-room window Daddy had put a bird-table, and on it each morning Billy-Bob put the crumbs from the breakfast cloth. At dinner-time Belinda scraped out the milk pudding dish and gave the birds the bits.

So you may guess that the birds liked Billy-Bob and Belinda, and sang in their garden all day long. They didn't like Wags so much, because sometimes, when nobody was looking, he climbed up on to the bird-table, by jumping on a flower-tub first, and licked up the milk pudding bits.

One day Billy-Bob saw a sparrow flying across the garden with something hanging from its beak. 'Look, Mother!' he called. 'What is that sparrow doing?'

'It is building its nest, Billy-Bob,' said Mother. 'All birds build their nests now, because it is springtime.'

'Oh, Mother! Will it build its nest in our garden?' cried Billy-Bob. 'What fun!'

'I want to see a sparrow with something in its mouth too,' said Belinda, looking out of the window.

'There goes one!' said Billy-Bob as another sparrow flew by with a long piece of straw in its beak. 'Oh, Belinda, let's put on our hats and coats and go out into the garden to see where the sparrows are building.'

So out they rushed. The sparrow was building a big untidy nest under the roof by the kitchen. It said: 'Chirrup, chirrup!' when the children watched it, and was not a bit frightened. It knew quite well that they were the kind children who gave it crumbs each day.

'Now let's go round the garden and see if we can find any more nests being built!' said Billy-Bob. 'It's so nice of the birds to build here. They know they are safe, for we won't take their eggs.'

They hunted all over the garden – but they could only find one more nest – and wherever do you suppose it was?

It was in the honeysuckle hedge that grew on one side of Belinda's own little garden! She saw a little brown bird fly in there and she ran to look – and there, tucked into the honeysuckle's fresh green twigs was the neatest little nest!

'Billy-Bob, Billy-Bob, come and see! The birds love me! They have built a nest in my own garden!' shouted Belinda, dancing up and down on her fat legs.

Billy-Bob peeped at the nest. It belonged to a small brown bird. It was a hedge-sparrow – not a noisy house-sparrow – but a little quiet brown bird with a beak like a robin's. She sat on her nest and looked at the peeping children quite unafraid. She knew they were her friends.

'Mother! Mother! Come and see!' shouted Belinda. Wags thought there must be a bone or a biscuit somewhere in the honeysuckle hedge, to make Belinda so excited and he jumped high in the air to see.

When Mother came to look, the little brown bird flew off her nest.

'Oh! Oh!' cried Billy-Bob and Belinda – for in the nest lay five eggs as blue as the spring sky! They were the prettiest sight.

'You mustn't disturb the nest,' said Mother. 'Belinda, you are very lucky to have a bird building in your own little garden.'

'They love me, they love me!' cried Belinda. 'Get down, Wags. They are my own birds, and my own nest and my own dear little blue eggs.'

Billy-Bob looked solemn.

'Mother,' he said, 'do you think the birds will build in *my* garden too?'

'They may not,' said Mother. 'You must wait and see.'

'Don't they love me as much as they love Belinda?' said Billy-Bob. He couldn't help feeling rather hurt about it. He did give them crumbs too – and once he had given them half of his biscuit.

'Oh yes, darling,' said Mother. 'Of course they do. But perhaps your garden hasn't such a good place for building a nest in, as Belinda's.'

'It has a honeysuckle hedge too,' said Billy-Bob. 'Well, I shall look every day and see if any bird is building in *my* garden. They must, they must, they must!'

But you know, they didn't! It was most disappointing. Belinda's little bird-family hatched out of the blue eggs, and became tiny little nestlings that opened wide beaks whenever the mother or father bird flew up with food.

'I have a bird-family of my own,' Belinda told everyone very proudly. 'The birds love me, and they have built a nest in my own garden.'

Billy-Bob was not at all happy about it. He and Wags hunted carefully every day in his garden, but never a bit of nest could they see – not even in the very thickest part of the honeysuckle hedge. Wags didn't really know what they were looking for – but that didn't matter. He hunted just the same, his short tail wagging nineteen to the dozen, and his red tongue hanging out of his big mouth.

'You can have half my baby birds, Billy-Bob,' said Belinda, when she saw how sad he was.

'No, thank you, Belinda,' said Billy-Bob, 'I like you to have all yours – only I do wish the birds loved me enough to trust me, and build in my garden too.'

'Billy-Bob, the birds don't think about that when they build in any special place in the garden,' said Mother. 'They like you both very much – you are kind to them. It was just by chance that they built in Belinda's garden.'

But Billy-Bob felt quite sure that the little hedge-sparrow hadn't built her nest there by chance. She had built it there because she loved Belinda.

'Now, don't worry any more,' said Mother. 'Go and get your spade and pail out of the summer-house and run to the sand-pit and dig. Make a house with stones for windows, and bits of grass in the garden.'

So Billy-Bob ran to get his spade and pail. He remembered where he had left them – in the summer-house at the back. He went in and saw his spade standing up. He looked for his pail. There it was.

But it was full of something. How funny! Billy-Bob bent down to see what was in it. And then he gave such a shout! He picked up his pail and walked carefully down the garden path, shouting: 'Mother! Belinda! Wags! Come and see! A robin has built her nest in my pail! Oh, do look! The birds love me too!'

Mother came running. Belinda trotted up. Wags galloped round, excited.

'Oh, darling!' said Mother, 'you have brought nest, eggs, robin and all! Take them back quickly to the summer-house, or the robin will be afraid and will desert its eggs!'

'It won't be afraid of *me*,' said Billy-Bob happily. 'It is my own little robin. Its nest is made of roots, dead leaves and moss – look, Belinda – it is a very cosy nest. I wonder how many eggs there are!'

'Billy-Bob, take it back,' said Mother. So Billy-Bob and Belinda took the pail back, carrying the nest, eggs and bird in it very carefully. The robin flew off when they put the pail down in the summer-house, and sang a little creamy song from the window-sill.

'There are five white eggs with red spots!' said Billy-Bob. 'Oh, I'm so excited. It's nice to have a nest in a honeysuckle hedge, Belinda – but don't you think it's nicer still to have one in my own pail?'

'Yes,' said Belinda. 'I do. The birds must love you a *lot*, Billy-Bob.'

Wasn't it nice for him?

Billy-Bob does some Gardening

ONE DAY Uncle Peter came to see Billy-Bob and Belinda, and he gave them two bright new pennies each. They were so pleased.

'I know what I shall do with mine!' said Billy-Bob. 'I shall go to the seed shop and buy some mustard and cress seeds. Then I shall plant them in my garden and when the mustard and cress grows I shall cut it and make sandwiches for tea!'

'I want to do that too,' said Belinda.

So Mother took them to the seed shop and they bought a pennyworth of mustard seed each and a pennyworth of cress. They were dear little seeds. The mustard was yellow and the cress was brown.

They danced home and Wags jumped round them in delight, because he did love to see Billy-Bob happy. Mother said it was a good day for planting seeds, because it had been raining and the ground was nice and wet.

So Billy-Bob and Belinda took their spades and went to dig in their little gardens. They each had a small square patch, with honeysuckle growing at the side. Billy-Bob dug his earth and made it fine and smooth. Belinda dug hers too, and Billy-Bob helped her to smooth it.

'I'll plant my seeds first,' said Billy-Bob to Belinda. 'Then you will see just how to do it, Belinda. You have to be very careful. Get down, Wags! You mustn't tread on my garden now!'

Billy-Bob began to sow his seeds in a very higgledy-piggledy manner. Do you know what he was doing? He was making a big letter B with them, so that the mustard and cress would grow into a B for Billy-Bob!

'I want to do that too!' said Belinda. 'I want a big B for Belinda.'

'I'd better plant your seeds for you then,' said Billy-Bob, 'because you can't write your letters yet.'

So he made Belinda's big B for her with the little yellow and brown seeds. Then the two children carefully covered up the seeds with fine earth, and ran to tell Mother that their gardening was done!

'You will have to wait for a few days before your seeds come up,' Mother said. But Belinda believed hers would come up the very next day and she went to look. Billy-Bob laughed at her, and Wags barked. They knew that Belinda was half a baby still, and believed all kinds of funny things.

'Let's go and play with Tommy the tortoise,' said Billy-Bob, who was really rather afraid that Belinda would begin to dig up her seeds to see if they had begun growing. That would never do! He had done that once, years ago, and his seeds had been spoilt.

Tommy the tortoise was a big old tortoise who had lived with Billy-Bob as long as he could remember. Every winter he was put into a box of earth and covered up. Billy-Bob put him in the gardener's shed, and there he stayed fast asleep till the spring. He woke up again then and scrambled round his box, making a great noise with his clawed feet until Billy-Bob heard him and put him out on the grass again.

Belinda did not like Tommy very much because his head went in and out in such a funny way under his shell. So Billy-Bob said that Tommy was his until Belinda grew big enough to like him.

Tommy was pulling at the grass. Wags barked at him and jumped round him. He always thought Tommy was some sort of live bones but he did not dare to bite him and see. Billy-Bob gave Tommy some lettuce leaves, and he ate one greedily.

'Billy-Bob!' called Mother. 'Put Tommy into the wired-in bit of the garden, or he will go and eat Daddy's new lettuces!'

So Billy-Bob put him there. It was a little piece that Daddy had wired off for Tommy – and sometimes Wags was put there when he was in disgrace. Tommy did not like being there. Wherever he went he bumped his nose against wire-netting!

Every day Billy-Bob and Belinda went to see if their seeds had come up – and one day they saw a great many tiny green things just pushing their way through the earth!

'Our seeds are coming up!' Billy-Bob shouted, and Mother had to come out and see them.

Every day they grew a little bit higher. It was lovely to see them. 'We shall be able to have mustard and cress sandwiches for tea soon!' said Belinda, who was never tired of running to her garden to have another look at the pretty green letter B growing there.

And then, oh dear, a dreadful thing happened! One morning Belinda ran to see her seeds – and who do you suppose was there, eating the mustard and cress as fast as ever he could?

MAY SMITH

Tommy the tortoise! Someone had left the gate open that led into the wired-in bit of the garden, and Tommy had wandered out. Wags was there, barking loudly at him, for he knew that no one must tread on Belinda's garden.

Belinda stared at Tommy and her nibbled mustard and cress in horror. Then she burst into tears and ran indoors to Mother.

'Mother! Mother! Tommy is eating my mustard and cress! Oh, Mother, it's nearly all gone. There's only just one bit of the nice green B left!'

Mother and Billy-Bob hurried out to see. And when Billy-Bob saw Tommy, he went very red – because, you see, it was Billy-Bob who had left the gate open!

'Horrid, horrid Tommy!' sobbed Belinda. 'I don't like your tortoise, Billy-Bob! Look what he's done!'

'Darling, he didn't know any better,' said Mother. 'He just saw something nice and fresh and green and came to eat it for his dinner. Billy-Bob will share his mustard and cress with you. Won't you, Billy-Bob?'

'I don't want Billy-Bob's, I want my own,' wept poor Belinda. 'Billy-Bob's won't taste the same as mine. Mother, give Tommy away. I don't like him.'

Billy-Bob didn't say a word, but he felt dreadful. It was all his fault. And now suppose Tommy had to be given away? Billy-Bob simply didn't know what to do!

'I'll look in my money box and see if I have twopence there to buy Belinda some more seeds,' he thought. But his money box was quite empty. Billy-Bob was very unhappy because he knew how bad *he* would have felt if Tommy had eaten *his* mustard and cress. He knew too that it wouldn't be a bit the same for Belinda if she shared his.

And then an idea came into Billy-Bob's head. It was seeing Mrs Blossom, the greengrocer, outside the front garden with her little pony-cart, that gave him the idea. He ran out and spoke to her.

'Mrs Blossom! I have some beautiful mustard and cress growing in my garden. I do badly want two pennies, so would you like to buy it, if I cut it for you?'

'Certainly, Master Billy-Bob,' said Mrs Blossom with a smile. So Billy-Bob borrowed Mother's scissors and went to cut all his mustard and cress. Mrs Blossom gave him two pennies, and he ran to Belinda.

'Belinda! I'm sorry about your seeds. It was

my fault about Tommy, because I left the gate open. I've sold my mustard and cress for twopence, and we'll go and buy some more seeds for you.'

Wasn't it nice of Billy-Bob? Mother let him take Belinda to buy the seeds, and they planted them together in another B.

'The B is for both of us,' said Belinda to Billy-Bob. 'Your mustard and cress is gone and so is mine – and this shall be between us. I won't be cross with Tommy any more now, because you have been so kind.'

And today they are cutting their new mustard and cress – it has grown into such a lovely big B! Don't you wish you could go to tea with Billy-Bob and Belinda and have a mustard and cress sandwich too?

Wags gets into Trouble

ONE DAY Wags was very naughty. Billy-Bob and Belinda took him down the lane with them when they went to look for buttercups for the dining-room table – and Wags suddenly saw some hens running about the road!

'Wuff!' said Wags joyfully, and his little black tail went wag-wag-wag. His long ears flopped from side to side as he ran up to the hens. He wanted them to play with him!

But the hens were frightened and ran away. 'Come here, Wags,' called Billy-Bob. 'You mustn't frighten the hens!'

But Wags thought that the hens wanted a game of touch-me-last, so he chased them, trying to catch the tail of one. He wouldn't go to Billy-Bob, though he heard him calling quite well.

And then Mister Greenfields, the farmer, came through a gate nearby and roared angrily at Wags.

'Get away, dog! I'll give you a beating if you chase my hens!'

Farmer Greenfields was a big tall man with a very red face and thick eyebrows. Belinda and Billy-Bob were rather afraid of him. The farmer caught sight of the two children.

'Hi, you!' he shouted. 'Call your dog off! Do you want me to give him a beating? I will if he chases the hens again.'

Belinda was frightened. Billy-Bob was too, but he didn't show it. He ran up to Wags and caught hold of him by the collar. 'Naughty, Wags, naughty!' he said, in his deepest voice. 'You'll be beaten!'

Wags put his tail down and followed Billy-Bob down the lane. His head drooped too, and his long ears almost touched the ground. He was ashamed of himself. He knew quite well he should not chase hens or sheep or cows.

'I don't like Farmer Greenfields,' said Belinda. 'He frightens me.'

'His voice is very shouty,' said Billy-Bob. 'I wonder if he is a kind man. I shouldn't like to be a horse or cow that belonged to him. Don't let's go down the lane by ourselves for a little while, Belinda. He might catch Wags and beat him, and that would make you cry.'

So they didn't go down the lane by themselves for a little while because they were afraid of meeting Farmer Greenfields. Wags soon forgot how naughty he had been, and his tail went up again and wagged nineteen to the dozen.

'Would you like to go and pick me some more buttercups?' Mother said, in a few days' time. 'The ones you got the other day are all falling to bits now.'

'We'll go and get some this morning!' said Billy-Bob.

'But I don't want to go down the lane to the field,' said Belinda to Billy-Bob.

'Well, we won't,' said Billy-Bob. 'We mustn't take Wags by those hens again. He might be naughty. We'll go over the stile and get into the fields from the other side. The sheep are there, and we shall see the lambs too. That will be fun.'

So they went to the stile with Wags. They climbed over and Wags slipped under. He was so pleased to be in the fields.

'Now, Wags, you are not even to *look* at the sheep!' said Billy-Bob, in a stern voice. Wags wagged his tail and kept close by Billy-Bob's heels. He meant to be a very good dog.

The children picked the yellow buttercups. There were such a lot of them. The fields looked like gold in the sunshine, with all the yellow buttercups shining brightly. It was lovely.

Suddenly Billy-Bob stood still and stared.

'Look, Belinda!' he said. 'There's a sheep outside the field, in the main road! It has its two lambs with it, too. Oh dear! Suppose a car comes by and knocks them down?'

'Let's go and chase them back into the field,' said Belinda.

So Billy-Bob and Belinda ran to the hole in the hedge through which the sheep and her lambs had squeezed. They squeezed through it too with Wags, and there they were, on the main road.

'Mother always says we mustn't go on this road by ourselves,' said Belinda.

'I know,' said Billy-Bob. 'Keep close by the hedge, Belinda. I'll try and get the sheep and the lambs through this hole again.'

But, you know, those silly frightened creatures wouldn't go back through the hole. They ran off down the road! Billy-Bob didn't know *what* to do! One of the lambs ran into the road, but its mother baa'd to it and it ran back to her side. Wags ran after them, and kept them well under the hedge. It was very clever of him.

Billy-Bob and Belinda ran after the sheep too. Soon they came to a little corner made by a hedge and a bush, and the sheep stayed there. Wags stood on guard and would not let them escape from their corner.

'Belinda, we must go and tell Farmer Greenfields about his sheep and lambs,' said Billy-Bob. 'Wags will guard them and keep them in this corner safely whilst we go.'

'But I don't want to go and see the farmer,' said Belinda. 'I am afraid of him.'

'I am too, rather,' said Billy-Bob. 'But we *must* tell him about the sheep.'

'He was horrid to us about Wags,' said Belinda. 'Why can't we be horrid to him about his sheep?'

'I don't know, but we can't,' said Billy-Bob. 'I wouldn't like those little lambs to be hurt.'

'Nor would I,' said Belinda. So she trotted off beside Billy-Bob on her fat little legs, her golden hair shining like the buttercups. They squeezed their way through the hole in the hedge and went across the field to the gate that led into their lane. The farm was not far off.

They went up to the farmhouse door. Belinda went rather red and so did Billy-Bob. Suppose Farmer Greenfields thought it was Wags who had chased the sheep and the lambs out of the field?

They knocked at the door. Mrs Greenfields opened it. She was a very smiley person and Billy-Bob was pleased to see her and not the farmer.

'Please,' he said, 'one of your sheep and two little lambs have got out on to the main road and we can't get them back. Our dog Wags has got them safe into a corner, but will you go and put them into the field again?'

'Well, if it isn't nice of you to help us like this!' said Mrs Greenfields, smiling all over her round face. 'Farmer! There's a sheep and two lambs out in the main road! The children say their dog has got them safely in a corner. You'd better go along and see to them!'

Farmer Greenfields ran off. Billy-Bob called after him. 'Please don't beat Wags. He is a very good dog, and helped us with your sheep!'

Mrs Greenfields made the children go indoors and sit down. She gave them two big glasses of creamy milk and two chocolate buns, hot from the oven. But Billy-Bob couldn't eat his till he heard Wags coming along, barking happily. Then he knew that his dog was safe and hadn't been beaten!

The farmer came into the big kitchen and smiled at the children. 'That's a fine little cocker spaniel of yours!' he said. 'He'd got those sheep safely for me! My word, he's a wonder. I should think you're proud of him! Thank you for all your help – it was kind of you to come and tell me. Would you like to come and help me get all the eggs off the nests this evening?'

'Oh *yes*!' said Billy-Bob and Belinda. There was nothing they liked better than holding warm eggs!

'Bring your dog too,' said the farmer. 'He's a fine little fellow!'

And now Farmer Greenfields and Billy-Bob, Belinda and Wags are firm friends. Wasn't it a good thing that Billy-Bob and Belinda tried to help him!

Billy-Bob goes for a Picnic

'WHO WOULD like to go for a picnic?' said Mother, one lovely sunny day.

'I would!' cried Billy-Bob.

'And I would!' cried Belinda.

'Wuff wuff!' said Wags, his tail wagging as if it would really fall off.

'Wags would too,' said Belinda. 'Oh, Mother, do let's go!'

'Very well,' said Mother. 'I will pack up a big basket of sandwiches and cakes and apples, and you shall go next door and ask if Peter and Patty may come too.'

So Billy-Bob and Belinda ran next door and asked Mrs White if Peter and Patty could come.

'Of course they may!' said Mrs White, smiling at Billy-Bob's red curls, and Belinda's red face. 'Peter! Peter! Here are Billy-Bob and Belinda come to fetch you for a picnic!'

'Oooh!' cried Peter and Patty and they rushed up to Billy-Bob and Belinda and gave them a hug.

'Our mother says she will take all the food,'

said Billy-Bob to Mrs White. 'And please don't put Peter and Patty into best clothes, because we are going to roll about the grass, and perhaps climb trees.'

'Well, I have some sugar biscuits,' said Mrs White. 'I think you might as well take some of those too, don't you, Billy-Bob?'

'Oh yes!' said Billy-Bob, who was very fond of sweet biscuits. 'I'd like those!'

'So would I!' said Belinda. Mrs White put twelve into a paper bag and gave them to Peter to carry. They got their shady hats and went back to Billy-Bob's mother. She had boiled five eggs hard, and cut lots of bread and butter. She had made two tomato sandwiches each. She had put in five big slices of lemon cake – and five red apples. There was a large bottle of milk too from Mrs Greenfields down at the farm.

'We're all ready,' said Mother. 'Come along! We will go to Bluebell Wood. The bluebells are over, but the woods are green and cool, and we may find some early foxgloves growing.'

Off they all went. Billy-Bob ran, Belinda skipped, Peter hopped and Patty hung on to Mother's hand and talked hard. Mother was the only one that really walked properly, but then, she had the basket to carry, and it would be dreadful if she hopped or skipped and spilt everything.

They went over the stile and across the field where the sheep and the lambs were. Wags was with them, of course, but he kept close to Mother's shoes, and did not look at the sheep at all, in case he frightened them.

Then over another stile they went and down by the hedge towards Bluebell Wood. The sun was so hot. The sky was as blue as forget-me-nots, and tiny clouds sailed high up like wisps of cotton wool. It was a lovely day.

When they were in the wood it was shady and cool. The birds were singing beautifully. A robin sang a loud song of welcome. It was dim and green and shady under the trees.

'Where shall we picnic?' shouted Billy-Bob, who was a long way in front.

'Find a nice place, Billy-Bob,' called Mother. So he looked about and found a good place, with soft green moss to sit on, and a tiny stream making a ripply noise nearby. Billy-Bob thought it would be just right to rinse their sticky hands in after the picnic.

'Yes, this is a lovely place, Billy-Bob,' said Mother. They all sat down and Mother opened the basket. She handed out a hard-boiled egg for everyone and a piece of bread and butter. They were all so hungry!

Hard-boiled eggs are lovely to hold. It is fun to pick off the shell and nibble the white and yellow inside. Mother let them all have a dip in the salt she had brought in a bit of paper. The tomato sandwiches were lovely too, and as for the cake, it was the nicest they had ever tasted!

'Now the apples!' said Mother. 'Dear me, you ought to grow big and fat, all of you, the way you eat.'

'There are some sugar biscuits too, Mother,' said Belinda. 'I can only eat one of mine. Can Wags have the others I don't eat?'

'Woof!' said Wags joyfully. Mother had brought him one of his own biscuits too – but he did like the sweet ones! They were much nicer!

'Now we'll play games!' said Billy-Bob, jumping up.

'Clear up all your bits of egg shell and that piece of paper, Billy-Bob,' said Mother. 'We'll take them back in the basket. The wood is so lovely that we really mustn't spoil it.'

'I'm going to wash my hands in the stream,' cried Patty. 'Oh, I wish we always had a stream to wash in! I'd never mind washing my hands then!'

Soon they were all ready to play games. They

wanted to have hide and seek first.

'Belinda, you hide your eyes,' said Billy-Bob. 'We'll go and hide. Mother will count a hundred for you. We'll keep calling cuckoo, and you must go towards the sound! We'll stay in our hiding-places till you come, and then we'll run!'

Billy-Bob, Peter and Patty ran off. Belinda hid her eyes in Mother's skirt and Mother counted a hundred. Then Belinda set off to find everyone. She heard a sound a good way off: 'Cuckoo!'

She ran towards it. It sounded again: 'Cuckoo! Cuckoo!'

'I can hear you!' cried Belinda. 'I'll find you in a minute!' She ran on again, looking everywhere for Billy-Bob, Peter and Patty.

They waited and waited and waited for her. But, you know, it wasn't their calling she had heard! It was a cuckoo's! And Belinda had thought it was one of the others calling, and had run off deep into the wood.

She was lost! She didn't know which way to go. She turned her golden head this way and that and called: 'Billy-Bob! Where are you? I'm lost!'

But there was no one to hear her. They were all round Mother, saying that they had waited and waited for Belinda and she hadn't come.

'Mother, I think she's lost,' said Billy-Bob.

'Oh, Mother, do come. I can't bear Belinda to be lost.'

'We don't know which way to go,' said Patty.

Mother looked worried. But just then Wags came running up and said: 'Wuff, wuff!' and Billy-Bob said: 'Wags! Go and find Belinda! Go on! Find Belinda! You know how we play hide and seek in the garden, don't you? Well, find Belinda, good dog, good dog!'

'Wuff!' said Wags and wagged his stumpy tail joyfully. He put his nose to the ground and raced off. He could quite well smell where Belinda's little feet had gone – and it wasn't long before poor Belinda, feeling very lost and lonely, heard the patter of Wags's feet and saw the little black dog come running up to her!

'Oh, Wags, you've found me!' said Belinda, hugging him. 'Please take me back to the others.'

So Wags took Belinda back to Mother and the others quite safely – and how pleased they were to see them both!

'You played hide and seek with the cuckoo!' said Mother, hugging her. 'And then Wags played hide and seek and found *you*! What funny games we have had!'

'You needn't mind about it any more, because it was an adventure, Belinda,' said Billy-Bob. So

Belinda didn't mind – but she was careful to keep near Billy-Bob after that, all the same!

Billy-Bob and the Kite

IT WAS a windy morning. You should have seen the clouds rush across the sky, and the chimney smoke bending over as it came out from all the chimneys around! The trees said 'Sh-sh-sh-sh!' all the time, and when Billy-Bob faced the wind it took all his breath away!

Billy-Bob liked it! He liked the wind to blow him hard. He liked to hear it go whistling by, trying to take off his hat. But it couldn't because Billy-Bob had pulled it right down on his nose!

Belinda was indoors. She didn't like the wind as much as Billy-Bob did because she was afraid it would blow her away. Billy-Bob ran round the garden and looked at all the flowers bending this way and that. It was an exciting sort of morning.

So it ought to be – because Billy-Bob and Belinda were going to a party that afternoon! And a day that has a party in it has to be nice from the very beginning – just to work up to the party! Billy-Bob was pleased and happy, and he hummed loudly as he ran.

The postman went up to the door and slipped some letters into the box. Billy-Bob didn't take any notice because he felt sure there were no letters from him.

But there was one for Belinda! It was from Auntie Susan, and what do you think was in the letter? A beautiful piece of blue silk ribbon to wear round her golden hair at the party! Belinda was so excited. She looked and looked at the ribbon and thought it was the prettiest piece she had ever seen.

'I must show it to Billy-Bob!' she said. And, without waiting to put on a coat she ran straight out into the garden.

'Billy-Bob, Billy-Bob!' she called. 'Look what I've got from Auntie Susan!'

Billy-Bob came running up, and Belinda lifted up the ribbon to show him – and what do you suppose happened? At that very moment the wind swept down and snatched the pretty blue ribbon out of Belinda's fat hand! It took it high into the air – over the hedge – far, far away!

'Oh! Oh! Billy-Bob! My beautiful new ribbon has gone!' cried poor Belinda. 'Get it, Billy-Bob, quick! It's to wear at the party.'

Billy-Bob squeezed through the hedge and looked all round to see if he could spy the ribbon

– but it was nowhere to be seen at all. Wasn't it a pity? Now Belinda couldn't wear it at the party!

Mother came out when she heard Belinda crying.

'The horrid wind blew my lovely ribbon away!' sobbed Belinda. 'Oh, I am so unhappy! I don't want to go to the party now I haven't got a blue ribbon to wear!'

'Perhaps I can find an old ribbon of mine,' said Mother.

'I don't want an old one, I want a very very new one,' wept Belinda. 'I was only just showing it to Billy-Bob, and the wind came and took it.'

'Never mind, Belinda,' said Billy-Bob, who did hate to see Belinda cry. But Belinda did mind. She went indoors with her face all puckered up, and Billy-Bob was left alone in the garden, wishing and wishing that he had been quick enough to catch hold of the ribbon before it blew right away!

He leaned over the gate, wondering if Belinda *would* go to the party now. She was such a silly-billy sometimes! He saw Peter coming down the lane – and Peter was carrying something so exciting that Billy-Bob forgot all about the lost ribbon and shouted to Peter.

'Hi, Peter! Is that your kite?'

'Yes,' said Peter proudly. 'I'm going to fly it in the field. You can watch me from the gate if you like.'

Peter was a little boy and the kite was big. Billy-Bob thought it was the finest kite he had ever seen. It was red, and had a smiling face painted on it. It had a long tail of red bits of paper that flapped about in the wind. It had a long, long piece of string wound round a stick for Peter to hold. It really was a wonderful kite.

Peter climbed over the gate that led into the field. He put the kite on the grass and straightened out the long tail, which had got a bit tangled. The wind found the kite and lifted it up and down as if it longed to get hold of it. Peter threw it up into the air – up it went – and up – and up – and up! Billy-Bob was so excited watching it that he nearly fell off his garden gate.

Peter unrolled the string and the kite flew higher. It did look lovely in the sky. Its tail waggled about and its face smiled and smiled.

And then a surprising and dreadful thing happened! The string broke! The wind blew so hard that the string snapped in half – and away went the kite by itself! Billy-Bob stared and his heart went thump-thump-thump. How bad the wind was today – first it had taken Belinda's new

MAY SMITH

ribbon – and now Peter's kite!

Peter was so unhappy. He tried hard not to cry, but the tears ran down his cheeks by themselves. He watched his lovely kite fly away over the trees. Then it dipped down – and down – and down – and disappeared!

Billy-Bob knew what Peter was feeling. He ran over to the field, climbed the gate and went to Peter. They stared at one another. Billy-Bob felt so sorry that he couldn't think of anything to say at first. Then he said: 'Peter, I'll go and look for your kite. It dipped down behind Bluebell Wood. It may be there somewhere.'

'But that's a long way away,' said Peter.

'Never mind,' said Billy-Bob, 'my legs are strong. You go and play in our garden till I come back. I'll be as quick as I can.'

He ran off. Over the field – over the little wooden bridge across the stream down by the hedge – and into the wood. What a long way it was! Billy-Bob's legs really did feel tired.

He hunted for the kite. He looked everywhere; and just as he was going to give up and come home, he saw it! It was stuck in an oak tree, half-way up.

'Oh!' said Billy-Bob, 'I do wonder if I can climb that tree!'

Up he went, and up. It was very difficult and twigs would keep sticking into him. But at last he reached the kite. He untwisted it from the branch, and tugged at the tail. It had been blown into a hollow in the trunk. Billy-Bob pulled it out – and then he suddenly noticed something else blowing on a nearby bough. It was something blue. It was – yes, it really was – Belinda's blue hair-ribbon! Wasn't that a surprising and exciting thing!

Billy-Bob was so happy. He untwisted the ribbon from the branch and put it into his pocket. Then down the tree he climbed, and, although his legs were tired, he ran all the way home for joy!

'Here's your kite, Peter!' he said, giving it to the delighted little boy. 'It's a good kite – it found something precious for me! Goodbye, I must go indoors now.'

He ran indoors – and how he called Belinda! You should have heard him. 'Belinda! BeLIND-a! BELINDA!'

'Here I am,' said Belinda, and then she saw her blue ribbon! 'Oh, Billy-Bob, my party ribbon! Now I can go to the party! Oh, I am so happy. Mother, Mother, Billy-Bob has found my ribbon!'

Soon Billy-Bob was telling Mother and Belinda how he had found it, and they both hugged him and said: 'You are a good clever boy, Billy-Bob, and we love you!'

Wasn't it an exciting morning?

Billy-Bob and the Pink Teapot

ONE MORNING Mother said that Billy-Bob and Belinda could go down to old Mrs Lucy's cottage and ask if she would let her have six new-laid eggs.

'But I don't like Mrs Lucy,' said Billy-Bob. 'She always looks so cross.'

'I don't like her either,' said Belinda. 'She looks as if she might eat me,'

'Don't be so silly!' said Mother. 'She is a nice old woman. She can't help her face being wrinkled. Take a basket and run along. It isn't very far.'

So Billy-Bob took hold of Belinda's hand and they ran off. Wags came with them, carrying the basket for them. He was clever at doing that. Billy-Bob had a ball in his other hand and he bounced it as he went.

'Perhaps Mrs Lucy won't be at home.' said Belinda.

'Perhaps she won't,' said Billy-Bob. 'I wonder how old she is? About a hundred I should think.'

'No, two hundred,' said Belinda, 'and I think her puss-cat is a hundred. Oh, Billy-Bob, I wish Mother hadn't sent us to Mrs Lucy's.'

'Well, you can stay outside the gate if you like,' said Billy-Bob kindly. 'Then you won't see her close to.'

'No. I'll come with you,' said Belinda, who always felt safe with Billy-Bob. On they went, Wags trotting behind them with the basket. He wasn't at all afraid of old Mrs Lucy and he couldn't think why Billy-Bob and Belinda made such a fuss.

At last they came to the cottage. It was a pretty little place with lots of flowers growing in the tiny front garden. Whiskers, Mrs Lucy's big black cat, sat on the wall washing himself. Wags dropped the basket and rushed at the wall with a loud and joyful bark. 'Wuff! Wuff!'

'Down, Wags, down!' said Billy-Bob, in a fright, thinking that Mrs Lucy would be very cross if she saw Whiskers being chased by his dog. But Whiskers took no notice of Wags at all. She knew quite well that dogs can't jump up on walls. She went on washing herself, and stared at the two children as they went in at the gate. They let Wags come in too, for he wouldn't stop barking at Whiskers.

They knocked at Mrs Lucy's blue front door. How they hoped that there would be no one inside!

But there was. 'Come in!' called a voice and the two children went in. Mrs Lucy was washing up. She turned round and looked at the children.

'Good morning, Mrs Lucy,' said Billy-Bob, holding Belinda's hand very tightly. 'Mother says could you let us have six new-laid eggs?'

'I'll go and see if the hens have laid enough for you,' said Mrs Lucy, and she dried her hands on a towel and went out of the back door into the garden.

The children stared round the little kitchen. It was a nice little place, very clean and shining. The three saucepans shone and the two kettles. There was a dresser and on it were some brightly coloured cups and saucers, some dishes, and two jugs. Right in the very middle was a big pink teapot.

'Look at the teapot, Belinda,' said Billy-Bob. 'It's got green and yellow spots all over it.'

'I don't like it,' said Belinda. 'It's ugly.'

'I expect it's very precious,' said Billy-Bob. 'Mrs Lucy has put it in the very middle of her dresser.'

'Wuff!' said Wags, suddenly. He had caught

sight of the ball in Billy-Bob's hand, and he jumped up at it. He did so love a ball.

'Down, Wags, down,' said Billy-Bob – but Wags wouldn't be still. He worried at the ball until Billy-Bob bounced it for him. Then he ran at it and cleverly caught it on the bounce.

'Oh, look, Belinda, did you see Wags catch the ball?' cried Billy-Bob, pleased. 'Isn't he clever?'

Wags brought the ball to Billy-Bob's feet and dropped it. 'Wuff!' he said, which meant: 'Again, please.'

Billy-Bob picked it up. He bounced the ball very hard indeed on the floor. It flew-up – and, oh dear, dear me, it bounced down on the dresser shelf, and knocked off the big pink teapot!

Crash! It fell to the floor and broke into three big bits! The children stared at it in horror.

'Look!' whispered Billy-Bob. 'Oh, look!' Belinda and Billy-Bob stood and stared at the pieces. Whatever would Mrs Lucy say?

'Wuff!' said Wags, and jumped up to lick Billy-Bob. But Billy-Bob took no notice of him at all.

'Let's run away,' said Belinda, in a shaky little voice.

Billy-Bob wished he could. But he knew he

couldn't. Daddy had told him never to run away from things. So he shook his head. Belinda tugged at his hand.

'Come along, Billy-Bob, let's go! Mother will tell Mrs Lucy.'

'Mother wouldn't like that,' said Billy-Bob. He bent down and picked up the three pieces. He fitted them together neatly. The teapot stood on the dresser and looked for all the world as if it were not broken at all.

'Shall we leave it like that, and perhaps Mrs Lucy won't see it?' said Belinda.

'Belinda, you are just a baby and you don't know what things are wrong and what aren't,' said Billy-Bob. 'We must tell Mrs Lucy ourselves. We couldn't possibly leave her to find it out. It would be very horrid and bad of us. Mother would be ashamed of us. You wouldn't like that, would you?'

'I don't want Mother to be ashamed of me,' said Belinda, looking solemn. 'I don't want to be bad and horrid. But I don't like being good and kind to Mrs Lucy in case she is very cross with me.'

'*I*'ll tell her,' said Billy-Bob bravely. 'It was all my fault. She won't be cross with you at all.'

He went to the back door and called Mrs Lucy.

'Mrs Lucy! Something dreadful has happened!'

Mrs Lucy came hurrying up the garden, six eggs in her apron. 'What's that?' she said.

Billy-Bob was very red in the face. He looked straight at Mrs Lucy and said: 'Please, I'm very sorry, but I bounced my ball and it broke your pink teapot.'

Both children waited to see how cross Mrs Lucy would be, and Belinda's knees felt quite shaky.

But dear me, what a great surprise! Mrs Lucy looked at the cracked teapot, and laughed joyfully!

'So that ugly, old pink teapot has got broken at last!' she said. 'I'm so glad. A friend gave it to me so I didn't like to throw it away – but it makes poor tea, and always looked so ugly, sitting up there on my dresser. That's good news, if you like!'

'Oh. Don't you *mind* then?' asked Billy-Bob, hardly believing it was true.

'Not a bit,' said Mrs Lucy, beaming at the little boy and girl. 'It was very nice of you to tell me about it, though. Some children I know would have run away and left their mothers to own up for them. Not you, though! Sit down a minute and I'll see if I've any sugar biscuits left!'

She took down a tin. It was full of sugar biscuits! How lovely! Billy-Bob and Belinda did enjoy them. They chatted away to Mrs Lucy and she laughed at all their jokes. She gave Wags a bone too. He was so pleased.

'Belinda,' said Billy-Bob, when they went home, 'Mrs Lucy is a very nice person – and we wouldn't have known how nice she was if we hadn't told her about that pink teapot. I'm glad I was brave! I always will be now I know I can be.'

Mother was pleased when they told her everything. She boiled them each a brown egg for their tea, and Billy-Bob thought the eggs that Mrs Lucy's hens laid were the nicest he had ever tasted!

Billy-Bob's Mother has a Birthday

ONE DAY Billy-Bob heard his Daddy say something that gave him quite a shock.

'What would you like for your birthday, dear?' Daddy said to Billy-Bob's mother. And Billy-Bob stood still for a minute and thought: 'Oh dear! I know I've hardly anything in my money box! And I *must* buy something for Mother, I must, I must!'

He ran to tell Belinda.

'Belinda,' he said. 'Whatever do you think? Mother is having a birthday soon – and we've forgotten to save up for it!'

'Well, let's save now,' said Belinda. 'Let's save shillings and shillings and shillings! Then we'll buy her a gold watch, and she will be pleased.'

'But, Belinda, we can't save all that in a little time,' said Billy-Bob patiently. 'Even one shilling is a lot of money. Let's get our money boxes and see if there is anything in them.'

So they got their money boxes, though Billy-Bob knew quite well that there couldn't be more than one penny in his, for he had taken all his money out not long before to buy Belinda's doll a new head.

Billy-Bob's money box was like a little house, and you put the pennies into the chimney, and unlocked the door when you wanted to get them out. Belinda's money box was a pink pig, and you put the pennies into his back, and undid his tummy to get them out. Secretly Billy-Bob liked Belinda's pig better than his house. It was so fat and round and had such a nice smile on its face.

There was one penny in Billy-Bob's money house and nothing at all in Belinda's pig, because she liked spending all her pennies. She thought it was silly to keep them in her pig.

'Now see, Belinda,' said Billy-Bob, 'if only you had put some of your pennies into your pig, you could have bought Mother a present.'

'But you put lots of pennies in your money house and you can't buy Mother a present,' said Belinda.

'Well, never mind about that,' said Billy-Bob. 'The thing is – how are we going to get some more?'

'I'll paint a postcard and sell it to Auntie Susan for a penny,' said Belinda, at once. She had a book of postcards that could be coloured, then torn out and posted.

'That's a very good idea,' said Billy-Bob. 'You do that, Belinda – but do try not to let your paint go over the line, it looks so messy. Now what shall *I* do to earn some money?'

'Once Mrs Greenfields gave you a penny for running an errand for her,' said Belinda. 'She might like you to go somewhere again.'

'Yes, she might,' said Billy-Bob, cheering up. 'I'll take my little cart down to the farm and ask her if she wants anything fetched. You get your paints out, Belinda.'

So, whilst Belinda painted a postcard, which had a wooden horse on it and was very pretty indeed, Billy-Bob trundled his cart down to the farm. Just as he was going into the yard he saw Farmer Greenfields, who was now a great friend of his.

'Hallo!' said the farmer. 'You're just the lad I want to see! Mrs Greenfields isn't well this morning, and I want someone to feed the hens. Can you do it?'

'Yes,' said Billy-Bob joyfully. 'I've brought my cart along – I will carry the corn in that!'

Farmer Greenfields put the pail of mash and the tin of corn into Billy-Bob's cart, and the little boy dragged it to the hen-run, on the other side of the farmhouse. How the hens squawked to see him, for they were very hungry! One even flew up on to Billy-Bob's cart and tried to peck the grain out of the tin. Billy-Bob thought it was a good thing that Wags was not with him, for he thought it would be very difficult to feed hens if Wags was about.

The hens were soon fed. Billy-Bob enjoyed himself very much. He took the empty pail back to the farmhouse. It was dirty inside so Billy-Bob carefully washed it under the pump in the yard. He put the tin back into its place too. Farmer Greenfields came along and saw the clean pail. He was so pleased.

'You're a good workman, Billy-Bob,' he said. 'How would you like to come along twice a day for three days till Mrs Greenfields is better, and feed her hens for her? I will pay you a penny a day for that.'

'Ooh!' said Billy-Bob, going red with joy. 'It's very kind of you, Farmer Greenfields. I would really like to do it for nothing, because I do so love feeding things – but, you see it's my mother's birthday next week, so I would be glad to earn some money for her present.'

'Splendid!' said the farmer. 'Come along at half-past five this evening.'

Billy-Bob sped home and told Belinda his great news. She had done two postcards, and had only gone out of the line twice, so Billy-Bob said they were very good. And when Belinda went down the lane to see Auntie Susan, what do you think? Auntie Susan bought *both* the cards, because she said they were so carefully done! So Belinda had two pennies already!

Billy-Bob told Daddy that he was feeding the hens for Farmer Greenfields, and that he was saving the pennies for Mother's birthday. Daddy said it was a fine idea – it helped everybody!

'You know, if you want a spot of work to do, old man,' he said, 'there's a nasty weedy patch in the garden that wants doing. I'd be glad to pay threepence to anyone that would clear it for me.'

'Daddy!' cried Billy-Bob in delight. 'Of course I'll do it!'

'I want to do it too,' said Belinda.

'It's very nettley and there are one or two thistles, I'm afraid,' said Daddy.

'I don't mind about that,' said Billy-Bob. 'If I get stung I know where to find dock leaves to put on the sting. I'll start this very day, Daddy.'

Well, you should have seen Billy-Bob and Belinda working at that weedy bed! Billy-Bob had a trowel and he dug up the plants that had big roots. Belinda pulled up the ones that hadn't. She got stung by a nettle, but she didn't cry. She just went red, and Billy-Bob rushed off to get a cool dock leaf and wrap it round her fat little hand. So it was soon better.

It took them all day to clear the weedy bed. Billy-Bob's barrow was filled three times with weeds. Twice he wheeled it to the rubbish heap and once Belinda did.

Mother was surprised to see them both working so hard, and she asked them why.

'It's a secret, Mother,' Billy-Bob said quickly, for he saw that Belinda was going to tell Mother everything – and that would never do!

Daddy was so pleased with the nice clean bed. He paid out three pennies at once. Then Billy-Bob ran off to the farm to feed the hens again. The farmer gave him a penny and Billy-Bob did feel rich that evening! Belinda had twopence – he had threepence and a penny – and another penny in his money box. 'That's sevenpence already!' he told Belinda.

For two more days he fed the farmer's hens, and Farmer Greenfields gave him two pennies more. Belinda earned another penny too for cleaning Daddy's pipes for him. She liked doing anything for Daddy. She popped the penny into her pig. He felt quite heavy now and made a nice jingly noise when she shook him.

'I've got threepence,' said Belinda.

'And I've got sevenpence,' said Billy-Bob. 'Seven and three are ten, Belinda – we've got tenpence between us. That will buy Mother a beautiful present.'

'Let's go and buy it,' said Belinda. So they called Wags and trotted down to the village.

'I want to buy Mother a watch,' said Belinda.

'That would cost too much,' said Billy-Bob. 'Besides, Mother's got one.'

'We'll look into Mr Philip's shop and see if he has any nice brooches,' said Belinda. 'Mother broke the pin of her blue one yesterday.'

So they looked in the shop window – and what do you think they saw there? Why, they saw a dear little silvery brooch in the shape of the letter M!

'M for Mother!' said Billy-Bob in delight. 'Look at that, Belinda! It's just what we want! We'll go and see how much it is.'

So they went inside. Mr Philip said the brooch was ninepence, and would be just right for a mother's birthday present. He wrapped it up for them in a nice little box. Billy-Bob and Belinda were so pleased.

'Now we have one penny left out of our savings,' said Billy-Bob. 'We will buy a red rose.'

So they bought a fine red rose from the little flower shop. Billy-Bob had to put it into an old jam-jar for the night and hide it out in the garden in case Mother saw it!

And the next day how surprised Mother was to find the rose in a little vase by her plate – and the lovely brooch in the box!

'It's just exactly what I wanted!' she said, when she saw the brooch. She took it out and pinned it to her dress. 'Doesn't it look nice!'

'It's M for Mother,' said Belinda. 'Everyone will know you are Mother now, because you have M on your brooch. How much do you like it, Mother?'

'Oh, very, very, very, very, *very* much!' said Mother, and she hugged them both. 'As for my rose I shall put it by my bed so that I can smell it all night through.'

Mother always wears the brooch, and she likes it best of all. Wasn't it lucky Billy-Bob and Belinda saw it in the window?

No Jam for Tea

BILLY-BOB AND BELINDA had been playing out in the garden. It had been raining in the morning, but now the sun was out, and the afternoon was lovely.

Billy-Bob wondered if it was tea-time. He felt so hungry. 'Shall we go and ask Mother when tea will be ready?' he said to Belinda. 'I feel as if I could eat a whole loaf, and a whole cake too.'

'And a whole pot of jam and a whole jug of milk!' said Belinda.

They ran to the kitchen door and peeped inside. Mother was there, wrapping up a parcel.

'What do you want?' she said.

'Mother, is tea ready yet?' asked Billy-Bob. 'I am so dreadfully hungry.'

'Tea!' said Mother, with a laugh. 'Whatever are you thinking of! Why, it is only half-past three. You will not have tea for another hour.'

'Oh, dear!' said Billy-Bob in dismay. 'What is there for tea, Mother? I do hope there will be raspberry jam.'

'I'm sorry, darling, but there's no jam at all,' said Mother. 'I've used it all in a pudding for Daddy, and the shops are shut today, so I can't get any more.'

'Oh, Mother!' said Belinda and Billy-Bob, in such sad voices that Mother really had to laugh at them.

'Well, is there any cake?' asked Billy-Bob. 'You said you might make some today, Mother.'

'Yes, I did mean to,' said Mother. 'But Mrs Thomas called in this morning, and I couldn't find the time to make cakes, when she had gone. Never mind – there is still a bit of seed cake left.'

'I don't like seed cake,' said poor Billy-Bob. 'You know I don't, Mother. Oh, it is horrid to think that just when I am so hungry, and Belinda is too, there is nothing at all for tea except bread and butter – not even any jam!'

'Woof!' said Wags, coming in and looking round as if he wanted his tea too.

'Go out, Wags,' said Mother. 'Your feet are dirty. Dear me, are *you* hungry too? What a family I have got this afternoon!'

'Can we come and play indoors?' said Belinda. 'I'm tired of being in the garden.'

'No,' said Mother. 'I want you to take this parcel to Mrs Lucy for me. It will do you good to have a little walk all by yourselves. Take Wags with you if you like.'

'Oh, Mother, must we go?' cried Billy-Bob. 'I do so want to stay here till tea-time. I don't want to go out.'

'Nor do I,' said Belinda. 'It will take such a long time to go to Mrs Lucy's and back.'

'Nonsense!' said Mother, giving the brown-paper parcel to Billy-Bob. 'Don't be such babies. Off you go and by the time you come back it will be tea-time!'

'With nothing to eat but bread and butter,' said Billy-Bob sadly. 'Come on, Belinda. Oh, Mother, she's going to cry.'

'Well, she must cry down the lane,' said Mother. 'There's nothing to make a fuss about. Goodbye, Billy-Bob, goodbye, Belinda, tea will be ready soon!'

Mother shut the door. Billy-Bob took Belinda's hand. 'Don't be a baby, Belinda,' he said. 'Let's be horses and gallop away. Then we shall soon be there and back.'

So two horses galloped down the lane, and Wags galloped too, barking joyfully. Soon the three of them got to Mrs Lucy's cottage. There were snowdrops out in the garden. They did look pretty. Billy-Bob knocked at Mrs Lucy's front

door and the old lady opened it.

'Well, well, well!' she said, smiling at them. 'So you've come to see me again. How nice!'

'We've brought you this parcel from Mother,' said Billy-Bob, and he gave Mrs Lucy the parcel. She opened it, and cried out in delight.

'It's the warm shawl your Mother promised to give me!' she said. 'Really, I think she's the kindest mother in the world.'

'Oh yes, she is,' said Billy-Bob. 'Well, good-bye, Mrs Lucy. We are going home to tea now. We do feel so very hungry.'

'Ah, I expect you'll have jam and cake and biscuits for tea!' said Mrs Lucy. 'Children are lucky nowadays. When *I* was a little girl I never had jam and butter together, never – and if we had jam, we didn't have cake!'

'Well, we are not so lucky today,' said Billy-Bob. 'Mother hasn't any jam, and there isn't any cake either – only just a stale bit of seed cake and we don't like that.'

'Dear me – and you are so hungry too!' said Mrs Lucy. 'Wait a minute – just wait a minute. I believe I have some honey left. I must look. I am sure you would like to taste the honey my bees make, wouldn't you?'

'Oh *yes*, Mrs Lucy!' said Belinda and Billy-

Bob, together. 'We *love* honey!'

Mrs Lucy went to her cupboard. In a jar there was some honey. She took a tiny glass jar and poured the yellow honey into it. She slipped a cap on top and gave it to Billy-Bob. 'There you are!' she said. 'Honey for tea!'

She looked at Belinda. 'I wonder if I can find anything for *you* to carry home too!' she said. 'A little surprise. Turn your backs and don't look for a minute.'

Billy-Bob and Belinda turned their backs to the door. They wondered whatever Mrs Lucy was doing. They could hear her rattling something – then they heard the rustle of a paper bag.

'You can turn round now,' she said, and so they turned round. Mrs Lucy held out a paper bag to Belinda. 'Open it at tea-time,' she said. 'Share the honey and share this too.'

'Thank you,' said Belinda, wondering whatever it could be.

'Woof!' said Wags politely, looking up at Mrs Lucy with his big brown eyes.

'Good gracious!' said Mrs Lucy. 'Do you want a surprise too? Very well. Carry this home and have it for your tea!'

She gave Wags a bone wrapped up in paper.

Wags picked it up in his mouth and wagged his tail so fast that it looked like smoke!

'Pick Mother a bunch of snowdrops out of my garden!' called Mrs Lucy, as they went down the path. 'There are some lovely ones by the gate.'

So Belinda and Billy-Bob picked twelve big snowdrops, and two green ivy leaves. How sweet they smelt!

'We'd better not be horses going back,' said Billy-Bob. 'I might drop the honey. Won't Mother be surprised to see the snowdrops and the honey!'

'And my surprise too,' said Belinda, hugging the paper bag and wondering what was inside it. 'I do like Mrs Lucy, Billy-Bob.'

They got home and opened the kitchen door. 'Wipe your feet!' called Mother. 'Tea is ready, and there is hot cocoa for you, for a treat!'

'Oooh!' squeaked Belinda, who loved cocoa. 'Mother! Billy-Bob has a surprise for you, and so have I!'

Billy-Bob gave Mother the snowdrops. How pleased she was! 'They are the first I have seen!' she said. 'We will put them on the tea-table, and although we have no jam, we shall have snowdrops to look at.'

'And here's another surprise!' said Billy-Bob,

and he gave Mother the pot of honey. 'Although there isn't jam, Mother, there's honey! Mrs Lucy gave it to me. We will all share it!'

'And I've got a surprise too,' said Belinda. 'I'm going to peep in this bag – and see what we've got!'

She opened the bag and looked inside. Then she gave a squeak of delight.

'Sugar biscuits! The kind Mrs Lucy makes best of all! There's one with pink on top – and two with white, and three with red! Oh, look, Billy-Bob, look, Mother! Six of them!'

'Well, you are going to have a lovely tea after all!' said Mother. 'What a good thing you were nice children and went to take the parcel to Mrs Lucy's for me. Come and sit down at the table.'

They all sat down. The snowdrops were in the middle in a little green vase. The honey was by the brown bread and butter. The sugar biscuits were on a blue plate. The jug of hot cocoa steamed away as if it were an engine puffing! It was a perfectly splendid tea!

'Oh, Mother, Wags had a surprise too,' said Billy-Bob, suddenly. 'We must tell him to have it. It was a bone wrapped up in paper!'

'Woof!' said Wags. He was on the mat. The paper was torn to bits – and no bone was to be seen! Wags had had his surprise already! He licked his lips. What a lovely bone that was!

The Big Naughty Boy

BELINDA HAD a baby doll called Amanda. It had a round baby face, blue eyes that shut and opened and a nice fat cuddly body. Auntie Jenny had given it to Belinda for Christmas, and Belinda loved Amanda very much.

Billy-Bob liked Amanda too, and when Belinda couldn't undo any of the tiny buttons Billy-Bob undid them instead. It was fun dressing and undressing Amanda.

Amanda was Belinda's very best doll. She played with her on Sundays and on any other special days. If she had a cold and had to stay indoors then Mother said she could have Amanda. The baby doll had a set of outdoor clothes, a nice dress with lots of things underneath, and a pretty nightdress for when she went to bed.

So you can guess that she was a very special doll indeed, and Belinda took great care of her.

One day Belinda said that Josephine, her everyday doll, had a bad knee and mustn't get out of her cot. So she asked Mother if she might have Amanda instead.

'Well, if poor Josephine really can't get up to-day, you had better have Amanda,' said Mother. 'But do take care of her, won't you, Belinda?'

'Oh yes,' said Belinda joyfully. She went to the shelf where Amanda lay in a box. She took out the baby doll carefully and hugged her. Amanda opened her eyes and looked at Belinda.

'One day Amanda will smile at me,' Belinda said to Billy-Bob. 'She always looks as if she is just going to.'

'Are you going to take her out in your pram?' said Billy-Bob.

'Yes,' said Belinda. 'If you come with me, Billy-Bob, Mother will let me wheel Amanda down the lane. So will you come?'

'Yes, I'll come,' said Billy-Bob, 'but we won't take Wags because he jumps up at the pram and makes it dirty.'

They told Mother what they were going to do. Billy-Bob fetched the pram and Belinda put Amanda into it. She covered her up and told her to go to sleep.

'She has got her eyes shut already,' Belinda told Billy-Bob.

'But she always does shut her eyes when you

put her to lie down,' said Billy-Bob. 'She can't help it. Her eyes are made that way.'

'She has very sensible eyes then,' said Belinda. 'They are like mine. When I lie down at night my eyes always shut themselves. Come on, Billy-Bob. I'm ready. Amanda is nicely covered up. She won't feel the cold at all.'

'I shall shut Wags up in the shed,' said Billy-Bob. 'Then he won't come. Wags, Wags, where are you?'

Wags came running up, thinking he was going for a walk. He nearly wagged his tail off.

'I'm sorry, Wags,' said Billy-Bob, taking hold of the little black spaniel's collar, 'but you are not coming this time. You will keep jumping up to see Amanda in the pram, and you make everything so dirty. You are going to be shut up in the shed till we come back. Then we will have a game of ball with you.'

Wags put his tail down. He did not like being shut up in the shed. It was horrid. Billy-Bob pushed him in and shut the door. Wags whined and scratched, but Billy-Bob would not let him out. The two children started off down the lane, Belinda wheeling her green pram with Amanda fast asleep inside, and Billy-Bob jumping on and off the grass edge that ran down the lane.

'I wish we could meet somebody,' said Belinda. 'I would so like to show them Amanda. She looks so nice when she is in the pram asleep – just like a real live baby.'

'We'll go right down to the duck pond and maybe we'll meet someone there,' said Billy-Bob. So down they went to the duck pond – and sure enough, they did meet someone there!

It was a big boy. He was throwing stones at the ducks on the pond. Billy-Bob looked at him in surprise.

'You mustn't do that!' he said. 'You will hurt the ducks!'

'Don't you tell me what I'm to do or not to do,' said the big boy rudely. 'You're a baby boy, you are, walking out with your baby sister and a doll!'

Belinda's eyes filled with tears. She had never heard a boy speak so unkindly before.

'Billy-Bob wouldn't be so horrid as to throw stones at anything!' said the little girl bravely. 'I think you are very unkind.'

'Is that a doll in your pram?' suddenly said the big boy, and he looked to see. 'A baby doll! Let me have it!'

'Oh, no, no!' wept Belinda, and tried to stop the big, naughty boy from taking her doll out of its pram. Billy-Bob tried to stop him too, but it

wasn't a bit of good. The big boy just gave Billy-
Bob a push and he sat down in the mud!

'Can your doll swim?' said the boy to Belinda.

'No, no, she can't!' cried poor Belinda.

'Well, we'll let her learn!' said the big boy –
and oh, whatever do you think he did? He threw
poor Amanda into the pond! Wasn't it a dreadful
thing to do? Poor Amanda floated there, her
white clothes spreading out on the water. Belinda
stood by the pond and wept. Billy-Bob took off
his shoes to wade into the water to rescue
Amanda – but it was much too deep. How that
big naughty boy laughed!

And then suddenly there came the sound of a
wuff-wuff just behind Billy-Bob! It was Wags!
He had managed to squeeze himself out of a hole
in the shed and had come tearing after the two
children. Billy-Bob shouted with joy to see him.

'Fetch Amanda, Wags, fetch Amanda!' he
cried, pointing to where the doll still floated on
the water. 'Quick, she's drowning!'

Wags was a clever dog. He knew what Billy-
Bob wanted at once. He just stopped to lick
Belinda's hand and then he splashed straight into
the water! He was soon out of his depth, but he
could swim well. The children could see his feet
paddling along fast, and his smooth black head

held well above the water.

'Good old Wags, good old Wags!' shouted Belinda, wiping away her tears so that she could see what Wags was doing. 'Oh, he's got Amanda! He's got her!'

So he had. He had swum right up to where the baby doll was floating, and taken her in his mouth. Then he turned himself round and began to swim towards the children again, Amanda held safely in his mouth. He ran out of the water and put Amanda down by Belinda. Then he shook himself well and thousands of drops flew off his black coat. They flew all over Belinda and made her wet, but she didn't mind a bit. She was hugging poor Amanda and telling her she would take her home and dry her.

Billy-Bob and Belinda had both forgotten the big naughty boy. But he was still there. He had watched Wags rescue the doll and he was cross. He picked up a stone and threw it at Wags. It hit him on the tail.

Wags turned round and growled. Belinda and Billy-Bob were surprised. They had never heard Wags give a proper growl before. Wags ran towards the boy, and the boy looked at him in alarm. He hadn't thought that Wags would be bold enough to run at him.

MAY SMITH M

'Make your dog go away!' he shouted.

Well, Billy-Bob did not want Wags to bite the boy, even though he had been very horrid, so he called him.

'Wags, come here!'

But Wags wouldn't come! He took no notice at all! He ran on towards the boy, growling hard. The big boy was frightened. He turned to run. He caught his foot in a tuft of grass and fell right over.

He was near the bank of the pond, and he rolled down it – and splash, he was into the water! Oh dear, oh dear! He soon got up, but what a wet and muddy sight he was, to be sure! Wags stood and barked at him.

'Woof!' he was saying. 'You've had a good punishment now! It serves you right! You threw Belinda's doll into the pond – and now I have made *you* fall in! How do *you* like it? Woof!'

The big naughty boy didn't like it at all. He shook the water from his clothes and tried to squeeze them dry. Belinda and Billy-Bob stared at him. Wags went on barking. The boy made a face at them and ran away. They never saw him again.

'Let's take Amanda home and dry her,' said Billy-Bob, putting on his shoes. 'I must dry my

socks too. Good old Wags! What a pity we shut
you up in the shed. This would not have
happened if we had taken you with us – but it was
clever of you to escape like that, and come and
help us just when we needed it!'

It was, wasn't it? You should have seen how
Wags wagged his tail all the way home!

Billy-Bob goes to a Party

ONE MORNING, when Billy-Bob came down to breakfast, there was a letter on his plate! How exciting! Billy-Bob opened it.

'Mother! I do believe it's an invitation to a party!' cried Billy-Bob, when he saw a coloured card inside. 'Oh, do read it to me!'

So Mother read it, and this is what it said: 'I am giving a party on Saturday. Do come! Love from Harry.'

'Oh! Oh! A party on Saturday!' cried Billy-Bob happily. 'I do love parties.'

Belinda stared at Billy-Bob, and her mouth went down at the corners. 'Am I to go too?' she said.

'No, darling,' said Mother. 'You are not asked. It's just Billy-Bob this time. He is older than you are.'

'But I am old enough to like parties,' said Belinda, and she began to cry. 'I went to one at Christmas time. I want to go too.'

'Don't say any more about the party, Billy-

Bob,' Mother said. 'Now, eat up your porridge, Belinda, and see if you can find the pussy-cat at the bottom of your plate.'

'Woof!' said Wags the dog, when he heard Mother say 'pussy-cat'. He looked all round but he couldn't see any cat at all.

'There!' said Mother. 'Wags wants to see the cat in your plate too, so hurry and find the picture there for him, Belinda.'

Belinda hurried, and she forgot about the party that she hadn't been asked to. Billy-Bob didn't say a word to her about it. He was very kind, and he knew that it would make Belinda cry again if he talked about a party she wasn't going to.

But when Saturday came, he had to get ready for it, and, of course, Belinda saw him!

'Why is Billy-Bob putting on his best blouse?' she said. 'Can I put on my blue frock?'

'No, darling,' said Mother. 'Billy-Bob is going out to tea, but you are going to stay and keep me company so that I shan't be lonely.'

'Oh, it's the party, it's the party!' cried poor Belinda, and she began to weep big tears all down her fat red cheeks. 'I want to go too. Why didn't they ask me? Don't they like me? Oh, I do want to go.'

Billy-Bob was sad. He put on his blouse and Mother did it up for him. Belinda cried all the time.

'Stop crying, Belinda,' said Mother. 'You are too little to go to this party. That is why they didn't ask you, I expect. You will go another time.'

But Belinda didn't stop crying. She went on and on, till Billy-Bob felt as if he would cry too! He was very fond of Belinda, and he hated to hear her cry. Her eyes were red, and her little button nose was red, and her handkerchief was as wet as a sponge. It was really dreadful.

'You are being unkind, Belinda,' said Mother. 'You are making poor Billy-Bob unhappy. He will not enjoy his party. What a pity!'

Belinda stopped crying. 'I w-w-want Billy-Bob to b-b-be happy at his papparty!' she said. She tried to smile at Billy-Bob, and he kissed her goodbye.

'I will try to bring you back a balloon or a cracker,' he said. 'I wish you were coming too.'

He ran off down the lane with his shoes in a bag. Belinda watched him from the window. She dried her eyes and tried to cheer up.

'I don't want to make Mother unhappy too,'

she thought. 'But oh, I am so sad not to go to the party.'

Billy-Bob soon came to Harry's house. He had not met Harry very often, for it was not very long since Harry's mother and father had come to live in Billy-Bob's village. But Billy-Bob liked Harry, and he was pleased to go to his party. A party was such fun!

The little boy knocked at the door. He was still feeling sad about Belinda. How nice it would have been to take her too! The maid opened the door and Billy-Bob stepped inside. Harry came to meet him.

'Hallo, Billy-Bob!' he said. 'I'm glad you've come. I say! We've got a conjurer this evening! Isn't that fine?'

'Yes,' said Billy-Bob, but he couldn't help remembering that Belinda had never seen a conjurer, and he did wish she could see Harry's conjurer.

'Conjurers are magic, aren't they?' he said.

'Oooh, rather!' said Harry. 'This one has got a magic wand. I saw it!'

'Goodness!' said Billy-Bob, in surprise. 'Fancy, a magic wand! I wish I could get hold of it for a minute! I'd wish a wish for it, I can tell you!'

'And what would you wish, Billy-Bob?' said

Harry's mother, coming out of the dining room to help Billy-Bob button up his shoes. 'I suppose you would wish for a bag of gold or a castle or something like that!'

'Oh no, I wouldn't,' said Billy-Bob. 'I would wish something for my little sister, Belinda.'

'What would you wish for her?' asked Harry's mother. 'Tell me.'

'Well,' said Billy-Bob, going red, 'it seems a funny wish – but I'd wish she could come to this party! She cried and cried when I went without her.'

'I didn't even know you *had* a little sister,' said Harry, in surprise. 'I would have asked her if I'd known. Mother, where are you going?'

'I'm going to ask the conjurer if I can borrow his magic wand for a minute!' said Harry's mother, with a smile. 'Wait here for me.'

She soon came back with a black wand with silver ends. She put it into Billy-Bob's hands.

'Wish your wish,' she said. So Billy-Bob, his face red with excitement, wished his wish.

'I wish Belinda could come to this party!' he said, and then he gave the wand back.

'Now we shall see if this wand really *is* magic!' said Harry's mother. 'I'll just go and give it back to the conjurer.'

Harry took Billy-Bob into the drawing room. Other children had come by now and soon they were all playing musical chairs. What fun! Billy-Bob did enjoy it – but all the time he was playing he was wondering if his wish would come true.

And suddenly, coming in at the door in her blue party frock, he saw Belinda, her face red with happiness, and her golden hair shining brightly.

'Belinda!' shouted Billy-Bob, rushing over to her. 'My wish came true! I wished you could come – and you *have* come! Do tell me what happened.'

'I don't know,' said Belinda. 'There was a knock at the door and Mother went out of the room, and when she came back she said: "Belinda, put on your blue frock and come with me," and I did, and she took me here! I'm at the party!'

'That wand was magic after all, then,' said Billy-Bob. 'Oh, Belinda, you are in time for tea, and there's to be a conjurer afterwards! It's going to be a lovely party.'

It was! Tea was simply glorious. There was no bread and butter at all, but there were currant buns with butter in them, banana sandwiches, half orange skins with jelly in, pink blancmange, chocolate buns and a very big cake with Harry's name all round it. Really, it was most exciting.

Beside every child's place was a little chocolate bear, and two crackers, one green and one red. There was a funny cap in one cracker, and a toy in the other. Billy-Bob had a clown's cap with black stars on, and Belinda had a yellow crown. She felt like a queen when she put it on. In the other cracker Billy-Bob had a whistle and Belinda had a very tiny black doll, which she liked very much. It had no clothes on, so she wrapped it up in her handkerchief, and Billy-Bob had to lend her his to wipe her sticky fingers on.

After tea, when they went back to the drawing room, they found that the chairs had been put into two rows. There was a table in front of the chairs, and a black cloth was on it. On the cloth was a black top hat, a teapot, some glasses, and the magic wand.

'It's the conjurer now!' said Billy-Bob and Belinda squeezed his hand in excitement. She had never seen a conjurer. They all sat down and waited.

The conjurer was a very nice man with the biggest smile Billy-Bob had ever seen. You simply wouldn't believe the things he did! He passed the top hat round for all the children to see, and they felt it and saw that it was quite empty. And yet, when he put it down on the table, and tapped it three times with his magic wand, what do you suppose happened?

Two white rabbits jumped out of it! Billy-Bob had never been so surprised in his life! As for Belinda, she just shrieked with delight and shouted: 'Oh, do it again!'

But the conjurer didn't do it again. Instead he took a lot of little coloured balls and said he wanted the children to play catch with him. Whoever caught one of the balls could have it – and as the balls were magic ones, well, it would be a fine thing to have one!

He took a ball and threw it to Harry – but will you believe it, it disappeared in the air! One minute it was there and the next it was gone! Then he threw one to Billy-Bob and Billy-Bob put his hands together to catch it – but it didn't even get to his hands, for it vanished like the other!

'Throw me one, throw me one!' shouted Belinda, and the conjurer threw her one – but that disappeared too. They all did, and nobody could *think* where they had gone to.

And then the conjurer walked up to the children, put his hand into a little girl's shoe and took out one of his balls! He took another from Harry's pocket and a third one from Billy-Bob's ear! Fancy that! Billy-Bob hadn't known it was there at all, and he was very puzzled.

'And now,' said the conjurer, counting his balls, 'I am one ball short. Where can it be? I ought to have eight and I have only got seven here.'

He stared at the children, and then he suddenly smiled at Belinda. 'Would you mind looking in your handkerchief?' he said. 'I believe my ball's there!'

Belinda was surprised. Her handkerchief was wrapped round her tiny black cracker doll. But she unwrapped it carefully – and there, beside the doll, was a red ball belonging to the conjurer! How *could* it have got there?'

'You can keep it for yourself,' said the conjurer. 'I expect your little doll will like to play with it!'

Belinda was so pleased. She wrapped the ball and the doll up together. What a lovely party this was!

The conjurer filled the teapot with water and then poured a glass of lemonade out of the spout – and then a glass of hot cocoa! And then, oh dear, whatever do you suppose came out of that quite ordinary teapot, which was only filled with water?

Why, three tiny goldfish! They swam round and round in the glass of water. Nobody could imagine how they could have got into the teapot.

Everyone was most surprised, and even the conjurer seemed astonished too.

'You never know what is going to happen when you start doing magic,' he told the children. He did a lot more tricks, and then said good night. The children played blind-man's-buff and a lovely balloon game – and then Mother came for Billy-Bob and Belinda.

They were tired but very happy. They each had their cap, their toy, and a balloon – and Belinda had her magic ball. And do you know what she did with it?

When she said goodnight to Billy-Bob she put the ball into his hand. 'You have it, Billy-Bob,' she said. 'You wished for me to be at the party, and I came. You used your magic wish for me – so now you must have my magic ball.'

Wasn't it nice of her? Billy-Bob still has the ball. He takes great care of it, as you can guess!

Billy-Bob Loses Wags

EVERY MORNING Billy-Bob took Wags out on the lawn and brushed his coat well. Wags had the lovely glossy coat of a spaniel, and when Billy-Bob had finished brushing him he shone like black silk!

One day Billy-Bob said to Mother: 'Mother, I think I will take off Wags' collar when I brush him. You see, I can't very well brush his neck when he has his collar on.'

'Oh, I don't think I would take it off, darling,' said Mother. 'If you forgot to put it on again, Wags would run off without it, and that would never do.'

'Would it matter if Wags went without a collar?' asked Belinda. 'Daddy has a collar every day, but he doesn't wear one on Saturdays, when he wears his jersey. Why can't Wags go without a collar too, sometimes?'

'Well, you see,' said Mother, 'every dog has to wear a collar with his name and address on, so that if he got lost, whoever found him would see his name and address and know where to take him to. Dogs are very miserable when they are lost.'

'Oh,' said Belinda and Billy-Bob. But Billy-Bob still wanted to take off Wags' collar.

'I really and truly will remember to put it back again always, Mother,' he said. 'I am quite good at remembering things.'

'Very well,' said Mother. 'Take it off each day and put it down on the garden seat. Then put it back on his neck as soon as you have finished.'

So the next day Billy-Bob took off Wags' collar, put it down on the seat and brushed Wags' neck as well as all the rest of his body. He brushed each leg, and he brushed Wags' tail. Wags liked it. He always stood as still as could be when he was being brushed.

Billy-Bob remembered to put back Wags' collar each day. He knew the hole that the point of the buckle fitted into, and the collar was just right, not too tight and not too loose.

Now one morning when Billy-Bob was brushing Wags, Belinda began to squeal with delight. She was down at the bottom of the garden. Billy-Bob wondered what was the matter. He rushed off to see.

'Look, Billy-Bob, look!' squealed Belinda.

'Here's a little baby hedgehog curled up under these leaves in the hedge. Oh, isn't he sweet!'

Billy-Bob took out his handkerchief and wrapped it round the tiny hedgehog, who was curled up into a ball. He was not much more than a year old, and his spines were a very light brown. Billy-Bob carried him up the garden to show Mother.

'We must give him some food,' said Mother. 'He is the tiniest one I have ever seen.'

So she got a saucer of food and the hedgehog lapped it up greedily. He put his funny little snout on the saucer, and made such a noise eating and drinking!

'He shall live in the garden,' said Mother, pleased. 'A hedgehog is a good friend in the garden. He will eat beetles and slugs and caterpillars – the things that gobble up our young plants!'

Well, do you know, Billy-Bob and Belinda had been so excited about the hedgehog that they had forgotten all about Wags! Billy-Bob had left him standing on the lawn – but when they came up the garden with the hedgehog, Wags was gone. He didn't come back again for dinner. He stayed away, and nobody missed him till tea-time.

Then Mother said: 'Where is Wags? Has he

been playing in the garden with you, Billy-Bob?'

'No,' said Billy-Bob. 'I thought he was indoors with you, Mother.'

'I haven't seen him since breakfast,' said Mother. 'I will go and whistle for him. Perhaps he will come then. It is his tea-time now and I have a big bone for him.'

So Mother whistled for Wags. But Wags didn't come running up as he usually did, barking and wagging his tail. Then Billy-Bob and Belinda called him in their loudest voices.

'Wags! Wags! Come along! Where are you, Wags?'

But no Wags came. Billy-Bob hunted all round the garden. No Wags was to be seen. Belinda climbed the stairs and looked into all the bedrooms, but Wags wasn't there either.

'Well, never mind,' said Mother at last. 'He will come in when he is hungry. He must have gone to visit a friend.'

So Belinda and Billy-Bob had their tea, and every time they heard a sound outside they thought it was Wags come home. But it wasn't. Billy-Bob got down from his chair and opened the door at least four times – but no Wags rushed in.

'I must just go and look round the garden once

more,' said Billy-Bob after tea. 'He might be asleep somewhere, Mother.'

Mother didn't think he would be, but she let Billy-Bob go. When he came in he was dreadfully upset. He held something in his hand.

'Mother!' he said in a miserable voice, 'look what I've found on the garden seat!'

He held out his hand to mother – and in it was Wags' collar.

'When I was brushing Wags this morning Belinda found the hedgehog, and I rushed off to see it and forgot to put Wags' collar on,' said poor Billy-Bob, with tears in his eyes. 'Oh, Mother – suppose he is lost – and hasn't got his collar on – and doesn't know where to go – and somebody finds him and doesn't know where to take him to. Oh, Mother!'

Billy-Bob burst into tears and so did Belinda. It was simply dreadful to think of Wags being lost without a collar. Dear old Wags, with his brown eyes and soft silky head – they had let him go off without his collar.

Wags didn't come back that night. Daddy came home and he was told about him. He looked quite solemn for he was very fond of Wags.

'It's a pity he's gone without his collar!' said Daddy. 'It means that no one will know where to

take him, if he can't find his way home again.
After all, he isn't much more than a puppy.'

Billy-Bob and Belinda went to bed very
miserable indeed. Belinda wished she hadn't
found the hedgehog, then she wouldn't have
called Billy-Bob. And Billy-Bob wished he
hadn't gone down to see the hedgehog then he
wouldn't have forgotten to put on Wags' collar.
They lay awake talking about Wags for a long
time, but at last they fell asleep.

In the morning there was still no Wags.
Whatever were they to do?

'We had better telephone the police station
here,' said Daddy. 'They may have heard of a
stray dog.'

So he phoned up the police station, but the
policeman there said no, they hadn't heard of or
seen any stray cocker spaniel.

Billy-Bob and Belinda sat in a corner and
looked most unhappy. 'Cheer up,' said Mother.
'I expect we shall find him soon.'

A little while later the telephone bell rang and
Mother went to answer it. It was somebody
speaking from the police station in the next town.

'I hear you have lost a black cocker spaniel,'
said the policeman. 'Well, we have one here.
Somebody brought it in this morning. It has no

collar on. What is yours like?'

'Oh, it must be our dog!' said Mother, joyfully. 'Ours has lovely brown eyes, a long tail, a black silky coat and a tiny white spot under his chin.'

'Well, would you like to come and see if this is your dog?' said the policeman. 'You shouldn't have let him out without a collar, you know. I'm afraid you will have to pay half a crown for him.'

'We will catch the very next bus!' said Mother. She turned to Billy-Bob and Belinda, who were listening excitedly. 'The policeman at Willdon says he has a spaniel there,' said Mother, 'a black one – and it must be Wags! But we must pay half a crown because he hadn't a collar on.'

'*I* shall pay that!' said Billy-Bob, and he went straight to his money box. Mother got the key and he opened it. He tipped out all his money – a whole shilling, a sixpence, a threepenny bit and eight pennies. 'Does that make half a crown?' asked Billy-Bob. Mother counted it.

'You are a penny short,' she said. 'I will pay that.'

'No,' said Belinda. 'I want to pay it. If I hadn't found the hedgehog and called Billy-Bob away from Wags he wouldn't have got lost without his collar. I have a penny in my purse. Here it is.'

'But you were going to buy a lollipop with that,' said Billy-Bob.

'I don't want a lollipop. I want Wags,' said Belinda. So Mother put her penny with all the rest, and Billy-Bob put them into his own purse. Then they got their coats and hats and went to catch the bus. Billy-Bob and Belinda were so pleased to think they were going to find Wags again. Billy-Bob had his collar and lead safely in his pocket.

'Was Wags locked up in prison?' suddenly said Belinda, looking very upset.

'Oh no,' said Mother. 'He is such a dear little dog that I am sure the policemen would be very kind to him and would let him lie by the fire.'

They got to the town and jumped off the bus. The police station was just near by. They went up the steps and saw a big policeman, without a helmet, sitting writing at a desk.

'Please,' said Billy-Bob, before Mother could speak, 'we've come for Wags.'

'And who is Wags?' said the policeman, smiling a big smile.

'Wuff-wuff-wuff-wuff!' suddenly barked someone in the next room, and two feet scratched behind a shut door.

'It's Wags, it's Wags!' shouted Billy-Bob and

Belinda, and they rushed to the door and opened it. And it *was* Wags! There he was, his brown eyes twinkling with joy, his tail wagging a hundred times a minute! He jumped up and licked Billy-Bob, and he jumped up and licked Belinda. He danced all round Mother till she felt quite giddy.

'Here's the money to pay for Wags,' said Billy-Bob to the policeman, and he counted it out. 'One of the pennies is from Belinda. Thank you for looking after our dog. I do wonder how he got here.'

'Well,' said the big policeman, 'he followed a butcher's cart from your village to Willdon, and he wouldn't leave the butcher's shop when he got here! He hid away under the counter till the morning, when the butcher found him – and, as he had no collar, he brought him along to me. So don't you let him out without a collar again – or it will cost you money each time you fetch him!'

'Oh, I won't, I won't!' said Billy-Bob, hugging Wags hard. 'You can't think how we've missed him. He is such a lovely dog.'

'I can see that,' said the policeman. 'I wouldn't mind having him myself – he's a fine dog!'

'Come along,' said Mother. 'We must catch the bus home now. Wags has got his collar on, so he will be all right. Put the lead on too, Billy-Bob, and he will keep with us then.'

Off they all went back to the bus – but, you know, Wags was so pleased and excited to be with his own family again that he ran round Billy-Bob and jumped, and got himself and the lead and Billy-Bob in a dreadful tangle. In the end Mother had to pick Wags up and carry him!

'I'd better brush him, hadn't I, Mother?' said Billy-Bob, when they got home. 'He looks a bit sawdusty, lying all night in the butcher's shop. You greedy little dog, Wags! Fancy running after a butcher's cart all the way to Willdon!'

'Billy-Bob, I'm going to be with you each morning when you brush Wags,' said Belinda. 'Then I can see if you remember to put his collar back again when you've brushed him.'

'I shall never forget again,' said Billy-Bob. And he never did!

Safe in Billy-Bob's Pocket

ONE DAY, when Mother was reading to Billy-Bob and Belinda they had such a surprise. They were both sitting on Mother's knee – and suddenly Mother's blue necklace broke and beads tumbled all over Billy-Bob and Belinda!

'Oh, Mother, look! Your lovely necklace is broken!' cried Billy-Bob. 'The beads are tumbling all over us. Quick, Belinda, catch as many as you can!'

'Oh dear!' said Mother. 'My best necklace, that Daddy gave me for my birthday! Find as many beads as you can, children; I must get it mended.'

Billy-Bob and Belinda jumped down from Mother's knee and looked for the beads. Some were on the floor. Some were in the chair. One was in the book, and one was in Belinda's shoe. That made her laugh. They picked up as many as they could find, and Mother said she thought they had them all. They were such pretty, sparkly blue beads. Billy-Bob fetched a tiny box out of the cupboard and Mother put them into it.

'I believe I've got one down my neck, Mother,' said Billy-Bob, wriggling. So Mother felt all down his back – it did tickle! And sure enough Billy-Bob was right – there *was* a bead down his back. Mother had to put her hand down his jersey collar and get it.

'Well, I really think we've got them all now, Billy-Bob,' said Mother, laughing. 'I must take the necklace to Mr Philip the jeweller, and ask him to thread it for me again.'

'Belinda and I will take it for you tomorrow,' said Billy-Bob, at once. 'You said we could go down to the village to see if Daddy's book had come that he wanted. So we will take your necklace with us. Mr Philip is next door to the bookshop. Your necklace will be quite safe in my pocket, Mother.'

'Very well, Billy-Bob. You shall take it for me tomorrow,' said Mother. 'Now, come back on my knee, and we will finish the story.'

The next day was rainy. Dear me, how the rain poured down! It was dreadful.

'I really don't think I can let you go out in this,' said Mother, looking out of the window.

'Oh please do let us go,' said Billy-Bob. 'We can put on our mackintoshes and sou'westers,

Mother, and our big rubber boots. It is such fun to go out in the rain.'

'Woof!' said Wags, who wanted a run too. 'Woof!'

'What a pity Wags hasn't a mac and a sou'wester and rubber boots,' said Belinda. 'Then he could come too. It's too wet for you, Wags. Your long coat and ears would get wet and muddy. You stay with Mother till we come back.'

Wags was sad. He went and lay down by the fire again, his long black nose on his paws, looking up at the children sideways from his big brown eyes. He hoped they would take him after all – but they didn't. It really was *too* wet!

Mother put on their mackintoshes and sou'westers. Billy-Bob's was green and Belinda's was blue. They looked very fine in them.

'You look like little fishermen going out to catch fish for my dinner!' said Mother, laughing. 'Have you got the box with my broken necklace in, Billy-Bob?'

'Yes, Mother,' said Billy-Bob. 'It's safe in my pocket.' He patted his big pocket. He could feel the box there. 'I will ask Mr Philip to mend it nicely for you.'

'Call in at Mrs White's next door and ask her if

she will let Peter and Patty come to tea with you today,' said Mother. 'It's so rainy you won't be able to play out of doors, and it will be nice for you to have Peter and Patty to play with.'

'Oooh, how lovely!' said Billy-Bob and Belinda, and they danced out into the rain. They went down the path and down the lane. They went up the path to Peter's house and rang the bell. Mrs White opened the door.

'Please can Peter and Patty come to tea to-day?' asked Billy-Bob.

'Peter can, but Patty has hurt her leg and must rest it,' said Mrs White. 'Come in and see her for a moment. She is very sad. Take off your wet mackintoshes and I'll hang them here in the hall. Patty will be so pleased to see you.'

They took off their mackintoshes and went in to see Patty. She was lying on the sofa and had a bandage round her leg. She had fallen down and hurt herself, but it was not very bad. Billy-Bob and Belinda talked to her and told her about their mother's broken necklace and how they were going to take it to Mr Philip's to get it mended.

'We wanted you and Peter to come to tea to-day,' said Billy-Bob. 'Your mother says Peter can, but you can't.'

'Oh dear, I *am* disappointed,' said poor Patty.

'I do love coming to tea with you.'

'I don't think I'll come today,' said Peter. 'I'll wait and come another day with Patty. She will be all alone with a bad leg if I go today.'

'So she will,' said Billy-Bob. 'Well, come another day, both of you. I will ask Mother which day. Now we must go because we have some errands to do.'

They went out into the hall. Billy-Bob took down Belinda's blue mackintosh and put it on for her. He buttoned it up because Belinda was slow at buttoning and usually did the buttons up crooked. Then Billy-Bob put on a green mackintosh and out they went into the rain, calling goodbye to Mrs White, who was upstairs making the beds.

They went to the bookshop first of all, splish-splashing through the puddles. It didn't matter because they had their rubber boots on. 'I know how nice it must feel to be a duck,' said Billy-Bob, paddling through an extra big puddle. 'They have rubber feet – at least it looks as if they have – and it must be nice for them to go paddling whenever they like!'

Daddy's book hadn't come but the bookshop man said it would come that afternoon and he would send it for Daddy. Then Billy-Bob and

Belinda went into Mr Philip's shop. They loved his shop. He was a clockmaker as well as a jeweller and there was a lovely noise of tick-tocking and chiming and striking going on.

'Good morning,' said Mr Philip, coming out of his room at the back of the shop. 'What can I do for you, young man?'

'I've brought Mother's broken necklace to be mended,' said Billy-Bob, and he put his hand into his pocket to get out the box.

But it wasn't there! Billy-Bob went very red and felt about all round the pocket. No – there was no box there at all. He felt in the other pocket. Nothing there either!

'Billy-Bob, have you lost Mother's blue necklace?' said Belinda, in dismay. 'Oh, Billy-Bob! It's Mother's best one! Let me feel in your pockets too.'

So Belinda put her fat pink hands into both Billy-Bob's mackintosh pockets – but no, there was nothing there at all!

'You must have lost it, young man,' said Mr Philip kindly. 'Go back the way you came and look into all the corners and puddles – you may see it.'

Billy-Bob and Belinda went out of the shop. Belinda was sorry for poor Billy-Bob. He looked so red and upset. 'I did think it would be safe in my pocket,' he said.

'Never mind, Billy-Bob, we'll look hard all the way and perhaps we'll find it,' said Belinda. So back they went down the road, looking everywhere – into every puddle, and by every kerb and even under the hedge though they didn't think it could possibly be there. And do you know, they went all the way home and didn't find the box with Mother's beads in it!

Billy-Bob stopped by the gate. 'What will Mother say?' he said to Belinda. 'She did love that necklace so. Daddy gave it to her. Do you think she will be very cross?'

'I don't know,' said Belinda. 'Shall I tell her for you, Billy-Bob?'

'No, I'll tell her myself,' said Billy-Bob, and he marched up the path. Mother opened the door and smiled at them.

'You haven't been very long,' she said – and then she saw their sad faces. 'Why, whatever is the matter? You can't have lost Wags, because here he is by the fire!'

'Woof!' said Wags, jumping up and licking Billy-Bob, for he knew that the little boy was upset.

'Mother, I've lost the box you put your

necklace in,' said Billy-Bob. 'I thought it was safe in my pocket – but it wasn't. It must have fallen out – and yet I've no hole in my pocket. When we got to Mr Philip's, the box wasn't there.'

Mother looked at Billy-Bob's sad face, and she simply couldn't be cross with him. She shut the door and began to take off their macs.

'Never mind, darling,' she said. 'You didn't mean to lose it. You are too little to take a precious thing like that to Mr Philip's. It was my fault for letting you.'

'I'm not too little!' said Billy-Bob. 'I'm very big, Mother. You're always saying so. Don't say I'm too little now.'

'Very well, I won't,' said Mother. 'Now don't look miserable any more. I'm not a bit cross, only sorry, like you.'

'I don't like you to be sorry either!' said Billy-Bob. 'Oh dear – if only my money box was full I'd buy you another necklace, Mother. But it's quite empty, I know.'

Just then there came a knock at the door. Mother opened it. Outside stood Mrs White – and in her hand was a green mackintosh.

'Good morning!' she said. 'Do you know what your silly-billy has done? He put Peter's green mackintosh on this morning, when he left our

house, instead of his own! They are exactly alike
– but Peter's has his name in!'

Mother took down the green mackintosh that
Billy-Bob had taken off. Sure enough, there was
Peter's name inside! Billy-Bob had left his own
green mac at Mrs White's house!

Belinda gave a loud squeal. 'Billy-Bob! If you
wore Peter's mac of course you didn't find the
box in it! It will be in yours, that Mrs White has
brought back! Oh, Billy-Bob, look and see!'

Billy-Bob took his mac from Mrs White and
put his hand into the right-hand pocket. He
brought it out again and there was the box with
Mother's beads in! It had been in the pocket all
the time, hanging up with Billy-Bob's mac at Mrs
White's, whilst Billy-Bob had worn Peter's!
Well, well, well, what a thing to do!

'Mother, your necklace is here!' shouted Billy-
Bob, dancing round in delight. 'Look! I hadn't
lost it after all! It was safe in my pocket all the
time!'

'Woof!' said Wags, joining in and dancing
round too. 'Woof!'

'Oh, how funny!' said Mother. 'I am so glad!'

'Can Billy-Bob and Belinda come to tea this
afternoon?' asked Mrs White. 'Patty couldn't
come to tea with you today, because she has a bad

leg, and Peter didn't want to leave her alone – so we thought it would be a good idea if Billy-Bob and Belinda came to us instead!'

'Oh, lovely,' said Billy-Bob. 'Can Wags come as well, Mrs White?'

'Yes,' said Mrs White. 'We'll have a special biscuit for him. Come at four o'clock.'

'Mother,' said Billy-Bob, when Mrs White had gone. 'Do you suppose Belinda and I could take the box of beads to Mr Philip's this afternoon before we go to tea with Peter and Patty? Or do you really think I'm too little to be trusted with anything so precious?'

'Of course you can take it,' said Mother. 'It was all a mistake – but never mind – I wasn't cross with you – and everything has turned out well! I have my beads safely, and Mr Philip will mend them – and you are going out to tea, and so is Wags. It is going to be a lovely day after all!'

And just as Mother said that the rain stopped and the sun shone brightly into the room. 'Even the weather is going to be lovely too!' said Mother. 'Now where's that box of beads gone?'

'It's safe in my pocket, Mother!' said Billy-Bob. And so it was.

Billy-Bob and the Cobbler

ONE DAY, when Billy-Bob and Belinda were out for a walk with Mother, Billy-Bob began to walk rather slowly.

'What's the matter?' said Mother in surprise. 'Why are you walking like that?'

'My shoe hurts me,' said Billy-Bob. 'Right at the toes, Mother. I think my feet must be getting too big for my shoes.'

'Oh dear!' said Mother. 'You grow out of your shoes long before they are worn out. Well, we must put them away and hope that Belinda will be able to wear them. She has the same shaped feet as yours.'

'Mother, I do wish I didn't have to wear Billy-Bob's old shoes,' said Belinda. 'I hardly ever have new shoes except party ones. I don't want to wear Billy-Bob's old ones.'

'They are not really old, Belinda,' said Mother. 'It is only that Billy-Bob's feet grow too fast. Billy-Bob, you shall go to the shoemaker to-morrow – Mr Knock, the cobbler – and ask him to make you a fine new pair of shoes.'

'Can I go too?' said Belinda.

'Yes,' said Mother. 'Billy-Bob shall take you if you hold his hand all the way.'

'Woof!' said Wags.

'Yes, you shall go too,' said Billy-Bob, who always knew what Wags meant when he barked.

So the next day Billy-Bob took Belinda's hand and they set off to go to Mr Knock's the cobbler.

He lived in a little house in the High Street. The front of the house was a big open window. On fine days Mr Knock slid this window up. On rainy days or cold days he put the window down. It was nice when the great big window was up, because then Billy-Bob and Belinda could look in and see exactly what the cobbler was doing.

Today it was fine and sunny, so the cobbler's window was up. Billy-Bob and Belinda looked in and saw him sitting mending a big boot. He was very clever. He had a hammer to knock nails into boots. He had a queer needle to sew with. He had strips of thick and thin leather hanging up on the wall, for Mr Knock cut out boots and shoes himself.

'Good morning, Billy-Bob, good morning, Belinda,' he said, when he saw the children. 'Have you come to have your shoes mended?'

'No,' said Billy-Bob. 'I've come to ask you if you will make me a *new* pair of shoes, Mr Knock. These I am wearing now hurt my feet. So Mother is going to put them away for Belinda.'

'Poor Belinda!' said Mr Knock. 'So she doesn't have new shoes like you, Billy-Bob! Well, do you know, in our family there were seven boys and I was the youngest – and I had to wear out old shoes, old coats, old socks, old gloves and old trousers! My, you never saw me in anything new when I was a boy!'

'That was much worse than Belinda,' said Billy-Bob. 'She only has to wear my old shoes. She's a girl, you see, so she can't wear my old clothes. She always has new dresses and hats.'

'She's lucky then,' said Mr Knock. 'Now come along in, Billy-Bob. I must get the shape of your feet right, or your new shoes won't fit you. Take off your shoes and come over here.'

Billy-Bob and Belinda went in at the door of the shop. It was an exciting shop. There were boots, shoes and slippers everywhere.

'Look!' said Belinda, in excitement, 'there are Mother's bedroom slippers. Have you been mending them, Mr Knock?'

'Yes,' said the cobbler. 'A heel came off one – now it's on again! You can take them home to

Mother, if you like.'

Billy-Bob took off his shoes. Mr Knock took two sheets of white paper. He made Billy-Bob put his right foot on one and then, taking a big thick pencil Mr Knock drew carefully all round Billy-Bob's foot. When the little boy took his foot off the paper, he saw the shape of his foot there! It was very exciting. Each of his toes was there. Mr Knock measured across the top of his foot too. He meant to make Billy-Bob a pair of shoes that wouldn't hurt him a bit.

Billy-Bob put the left foot on the other bit of paper and the cobbler drew that too and measured it carefully. Then he put the pieces of paper, with Billy-Bob's name on, away on a shelf.

'I'll begin the shoes tomorrow,' he said.

'I should like you to draw round *my* feet too,' said Belinda to the cobbler. She began to unbutton her shoe, but just then someone else came into the shop with some shoes to mend. Billy-Bob did up Belinda's shoe.

'Mr Knock hasn't time to draw round your feet too,' he said. 'Besides, he only does it when he is going to make shoes for you.'

Belinda was disappointed. 'I do think I might have had my feet drawn round, even though I'm not having new shoes,' she said, and she looked so much as if she were going to cry that Billy-Bob hurried her out of the shop at once.

'Where's Wags?' he said, and Belinda looked round for him and forgot to cry. 'There he is!' said Billy-Bob, 'in the butcher's shop as usual. Wags, Wags, come here!'

The next day Billy-Bob, Belinda and Mother went for a walk, and they passed the cobbler's shop. 'Go in and ask Mr Knock for my slippers,' Mother said to Billy-Bob. 'You forgot to bring them home yesterday after all!'

Billy-Bob went into the shop. Belinda went with him. She was carrying Amanda, her best doll, for a treat. Mr Knock gave Billy-Bob Mother's slippers and then looked at Amanda. 'My word!' he said, 'that's a fine doll you've got! What sort of shoes does she wear?'

'She doesn't wear any,' said Belinda. 'She is a baby doll. She has socks. I shall buy her some shoes when she grows bigger.'

Mr Knock looked at Amanda's feet. They were nice fat feet, soft and pink. Belinda suddenly had a fine idea. 'Mr Knock, oh, Mr Knock, will you draw round Amanda's feet for me like you did Billy-Bob's?' she cried. 'I would so like to see what Amanda's feet are like when you draw them on paper!'

Mr Knock took a sheet of paper and made Belinda stand Amanda on it. Then he drew carefully round the doll's feet. What funny little feet she had! Belinda was pleased. 'Thank you very much,' she said. 'Now I know what Amanda's feet are like on paper. Oh, Amanda, you are very grown-up to have your feet drawn round!'

Then Mother called them and they ran out. They did not go to Mr Knock's shop for a whole week after that, and then he sent a message to say that Billy-Bob's shoes were ready.

'You shall go and fetch them today,' Mother said. 'You can wear them home.'

'I wish *I* had new shoes to wear,' began Belinda. 'I wish...'

'Don't grumble, Belinda,' said Billy-Bob. 'New shoes cost a lot of money. It is a good thing you can save Mother money by wearing my old shoes. Mother can buy lots of nice things with the money you save her.'

'Oh,' said Belinda, and she didn't say any more. She was pleased that she could save Mother money. She and Billy-Bob put on their hats and coats and went to fetch the new shoes. Mother said Belinda might take Amanda in the pram, as Josephine, the other doll, had fallen into the bath the night before and was still drying in front of the fire. So Belinda put Amanda into the pram, covered her up and set off down the lane with Billy-Bob. When they got to Mr Knock's he had his window wide open, for it was a lovely day. He smiled at the children.

'Come to fetch your new shoes?' he said. 'My word, they are beauties! Come in and try them on.'

Billy-Bob and Belinda went in. Belinda left her pram outside. Mr Knock took down a pair of strong lace shoes from a shelf – Billy-Bob's new shoes! Oh, how pleased the little boy was!

'They are the nicest ones I've ever had,' he said. 'Oh, they do feel cosy and comfortable. There is plenty of room for my toes. How clever you are, Mr Knock! I wish I could make shoes like you. Aren't they lovely and big! And the laces are made of leather, like Daddy's. Thank you so much for making me such nice shoes, Mr Knock.'

Belinda stood and looked at Billy-Bob's lovely new shoes. But she didn't say a word. She didn't mean to grumble any more. Mr Knock looked at her and smiled.

'Don't you wish you had new shoes like that?' he said.

'Yes,' said Belinda, 'but Billy-Bob says it saves money if I wear his old ones.'

'What a nice little girl you are!' said Mr Knock. 'And do you know I've got a surprise for a nice little girl – and here *you* come walking into my shop! Isn't that lucky?'

'Oh,' said Belinda, in excitement. 'What sort of a surprise?'

'Fetch your dolly in and I'll show you,' said Mr Knock. So Belinda ran to her pram and fetched Amanda. And when she got back, whatever do you think! Mr Knock had taken out of a drawer a pair of tiny red shoes with tiny red buttons! Belinda stared at them in delight.

'These are for your doll,' said Mr Knock. 'If *you* can't have new shoes, your dolly can! She doesn't have to wear shoes belonging to a bigger doll, does she?'

'Oh no!' squealed Belinda, taking up the tiny shoes and fitting them on to Amanda's feet. 'No other doll has shoes like these! Oh, Mr Knock, do look! They fit beautifully. How *did* you guess the size of Amanda's little feet?'

'He drew round them the other day!' cried Billy-Bob, 'and then he made the shoes! Oh, Belinda, what a lovely surprise for you! It's better than having shoes yourself!'

'Oh, I'm so proud of Amanda's shoes!' said Belinda happily. 'Thank you, Mr Knock. I'm going home to show Mother now.'

They went home. Billy-Bob was so proud of his new shoes, and as for Belinda, she kept Amanda's dress turned right back so that everyone could see the new red shoes!

And now Amanda isn't a baby doll any more because Mother said she really must have short dresses to show off her beautiful red shoes. So Mother made her a pink dress and a pink hat. Wasn't Belinda lucky?

The New Little Kitten

BILLY-BOB AND BELINDA had two pets – Wags their dog, and Tommy their tortoise. Tommy was fun in the summertime when he put his head in and out of his shell – but he wasn't much fun in the winter because then Mother put him into a box, and popped him on a shelf in the shed to go to sleep.

'He likes to sleep all through the cold days, you see,' Mother said. 'He will not wake up until the spring.'

'I wish we had a cat,' said Billy-Bob.

'Wags wouldn't like a kitten,' said Mother, 'and it will never do to bring a grown-up cat here, for it might fly at Wags and scratch his lovely brown eyes.'

'How do you know Wags wouldn't like a kitten, Mother?' said Belinda. 'I think Wags would love one.'

'Oh, Wags is quite enough for you,' Mother said. 'If you want to play with a cat you can go and play with Peter's next door. He is always ready for a game.'

Down at Mrs Blossom the grocer's was a little tabby kitten. Billy-Bob and Belinda always peeped into the shop to see if it was there. It would chase any bit of paper and if it had no paper to run after it would go round and round after its own tail. Billy-Bob and Belinda watched Mrs Blossom's kitten for a long time whenever they passed.

'I do wish we had a kitten like that,' said Billy-Bob. 'Oh, Wags, I wish you liked kittens. I think Mother is right – you would not be very kind to a little kitten, because yesterday you chased Mrs Blossom's tabby one, and frightened it.'

'Wuff!' said Wags and wagged his tail. He meant that he was always ready to chase a cat. But Billy-Bob did not like him to. Nor did Belinda.

One day Mother asked Billy-Bob to go with Belinda and Wags to Mr Lundy's cottage and leave a note in his letterbox. 'You need not knock at the door,' she said. 'Just push the note into the letterbox and come away.'

Mother knew that the children did not like Mr Lundy very much, because once he had chased Wags with a stick. Wags had run into Mr Lundy's garden and trodden on his crocuses, and Mr Lundy had been very angry.

'He didn't get Wags,' said Belinda, remembering, 'but he had a very big stick. Perhaps we had better leave Wags at home, Mother, this time. Mr Lundy might be in his garden again, and he mustn't chase Wags.'

'You needn't worry about that,' said Mother. 'Mr Lundy is quite nice really. Put Wags on a lead and then he won't run into anybody's garden today.'

So Billy-Bob fetched Wags's lead and fastened it to his collar. Wags wagged his tail hard. He didn't mind having a lead on so long as he could go out with Billy-Bob and Belinda! They all set off, Billy-Bob carrying Mother's note in one hand and holding the lead in the other.

Wags was quite good. He trotted along by Billy-Bob happily, sniffing at the hedges as he passed. Belinda was surprised to think there were so many smells for Wags to sniff at. He always seemed to find such a lot.

Just before they came to Mr Lundy's cottage Wags pulled so hard at the lead that Billy-Bob had to stop. Wags was trying to get right into the hedge! He had smelt something there and he wanted to see what it was.

'Come on, Wags, come on,' said Billy-Bob, but Wags simply wouldn't come. Belinda tried to see what Wags was sniffing at – and she gave a squeal of surprise.

'Billy-Bob! Look! There are some eggs there in a little hole, with dead leaves all round them. They look like the eggs we have for breakfast!'

Billy-Bob squeezed under the hedge and looked. Yes, Belinda was right. There were five eggs there, hen's eggs, in a neat little pile.

'Oh, fancy Wags smelling there were eggs there!' said Billy-Bob, surprised. 'Good dog, Wags!'

'Woof!' said Wags and tried to get at the eggs – but Billy-Bob pulled him back. 'No – you'll break them!' he said. 'Belinda, these eggs must belong to Mr Lundy. This is the hedge that goes round his garden. He keeps hens because I can hear them clucking. I expect one got out and laid her eggs here. We ought to take them to Mr Lundy.'

'I don't want to,' said Belinda. 'I don't want to knock at his door and see him.'

'Well, I will, then,' said Billy-Bob. 'Let's tie Wags to this branch in the hedge, Belinda. Then he won't come with us. I'll carry three of the eggs and you carry two.'

He picked up two of the eggs and gave them to Belinda. She held one in each hand. They felt nice and smooth. She liked them. Billy-Bob picked up the third egg with his left hand and tried to pick up two with his right hand. He could only just manage to take two in one hand, for the eggs were big and his hand was rather small.

'Come on,' he said to Belinda. 'You can stand at the gate, if you like, and not go in. I'll go and knock and tell Mr Lundy, and then I'll fetch the eggs you've got.'

Belinda and Billy-Bob went along by the hedge to Mr Lundy's gate – and do you know, as Billy-Bob was trying to open it, one of the eggs he was carrying in his right hand fell to the ground – and broke!

Belinda and Billy-Bob looked at it. It lay on the ground with the yellow yolk coming out – just like the picture of Humpty Dumpty in their picture book.

'It's broken,' said Belinda.

'Oh dear,' said Billy-Bob. 'I wonder if Mr Lundy will mind.'

'Don't tell him, Billy-Bob,' said Belinda. 'He doesn't know how many eggs we found.'

'Oh, Belinda, I shall have to tell him,' said Billy-Bob. 'Supposing he asked. Besides, we shall tell Mother when we go home, and Mother would be sorry we hadn't told Mr Lundy the truth. Oh dear! I wish I hadn't tried to carry two eggs in one hand!'

'I shall stay here,' said Belinda, but then she changed her mind. 'No, I won't. I'll come in too.'

So she and Billy-Bob went in at the gate and walked up the path to Mr Lundy's front door. Billy-Bob knocked – rat-tat!

Mr Lundy opened the door himself. 'Hallo,' he said. 'And what do *you* want?'

'I've come to bring you a note from Mother,' said Billy-Bob. 'And on the way we found some hen's eggs under your hedge, Mr Lundy.'

'There!' said Mr Lundy. 'I knew one of my hens had been laying away. So you found the eggs, did you, and brought them along?'

'Yes,' said Billy-Bob. 'I've got two and Belinda has two.'

'So there were four,' said Mr Lundy and he took the four eggs. 'Thank you very much.'

'Well,' said Billy-Bob, going very red. 'There were five.'

'Oh,' said Mr Lundy, 'I suppose you left the other one because you couldn't carry it. Very sensible of you.'

'No, I didn't leave it,' said Billy-Bob. 'I tried to carry it, and when I opened your gate it fell out of my hand and broke. I'm really very sorry.'

'Very nice of you to tell me,' said Mr Lundy, patting Billy-Bob on the back, and making his eyes twinkle so much that Belinda couldn't help staring at him. 'Good boy! You didn't need to tell me but you did. That's the thing to do! Now where's your mother's note?'

Billy-Bob felt in his pocket and took out the note. 'Thank you,' said Mr Lundy. 'Now I wonder if you'd like to come and see two puppies and three kittens I've got out in the garden. They are very funny when they play with one another! Come along and see them.'

The children went through the house and out into the garden at the back. There they saw two brown puppies playing with two black kittens. They rolled each other over, and they were so funny that Billy-Bob and Belinda laughed loudly.

'But you said there were three kittens,' said Billy-Bob, looking all round.

'So there were,' said Mr Lundy. 'Now where's the other one? It's the prettiest of the lot, because it has golden eyes. It hasn't a home yet, and the other two have. Would *you* like to have it?'

'Oh!' said Billy-Bob and Belinda both together, their eyes shining with joy. 'I wonder if Mother would let us. She always said Wags wouldn't like a kitten.'

'Is that your dog over there?' said Mr Lundy, pointing to a corner of his garden. And do you know, Wags had pulled his lead loose from the branch and had got into Mr Lundy's garden and was sniffing all round it! Wasn't he dreadful?

'Oh dear, I'm afraid it *is* Wags,' said Billy-Bob, in dismay. 'I'm so sorry, Mr Lundy. We tied him up so that he shouldn't come in.'

'Never mind,' said Mr Lundy. 'He doesn't seem to be doing any harm. Let's look for the other kitten.'

'Wags has got something in his mouth,' said Belinda. 'I hope he isn't eating anything of yours, Mr Lundy.'

'Wags, come here!' called Billy-Bob. Wags came out of the ditch where he had been sniffing about and ran to Billy-Bob, carrying something gently in his mouth.

'Oh, it's the lost kitten, it's the lost kitten,' cried Belinda, jumping up and down. 'Oh, Wags, you clever dog!'

'Why, the kitten is wet and cold,' said Mr Lundy, picking it up. Wags had laid it gently down at his feet and had been licking it carefully. 'It must have fallen into the ditch of water and Wags smelt it or heard it and fetched it out. Poor little mite!'

'Well, if Wags did that he must like kittens!' said Billy-Bob, thinking hard. 'Mr Lundy, do you suppose Wags would like that kitten to live with him at our house?'

'I'm sure of it!' said Mr Lundy, putting the kitten inside his coat. 'A dog isn't as gentle as Wags was with a kitten unless he is the kind that likes other creatures about him. Besides, all these kittens are used to dogs. This one will be a good playfellow for Wags – and for you too. You go home and ask your mother and see what she says – and if she says yes, come along and fetch the kitten when it's dry and warm again!'

Off ran Billy-Bob and Belinda in excitement. Mother was surprised to see their faces when they got home, they were so red and excited. Billy-Bob told Mother everything, and Mother listened hard.

'Billy-Bob, you deserve to have the kitten,' she said. 'It was nice of you to take the eggs to Mr Lundy when you were half afraid of him – and brave of you to tell him that you had broken one – and it was sweet of Wags to be so gentle with the kitten he found. I am sure he would like it to play with. So this afternoon you can go and fetch it in a basket.'

'Oh, thank you, Mother!' shouted the

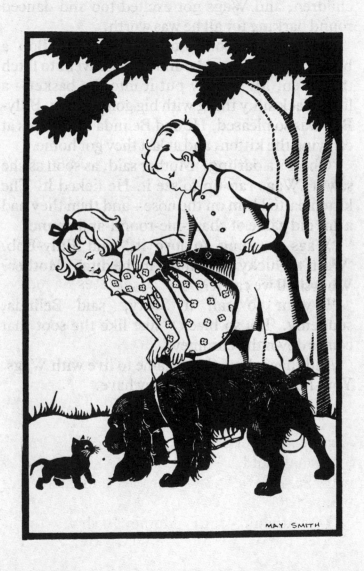

MAY SMITH

children, and Wags got excited too and danced round barking for all he was worth.

In the afternoon Mother gave Billy-Bob a basket with a lid and he and Belinda went to fetch the kitten. Mr Lundy put it into the basket – a little black silky thing with big golden eyes. Billy-Bob was so pleased. He and Belinda took turns at carrying the kitten, and at last they got home.

'Oh, it's a darling!' Mother said, as soon as she saw it. Wags ran up to see it. He licked it. The kitten patted him on the nose – and then they had a fine old game of chase-me-round-and-round.

'Wags is going to love it,' said Billy-Bob. 'Wasn't it lucky he found it in the ditch, Mother? What shall we call it?'

'I want to call it Sooty,' said Belinda, suddenly. 'It's so black – just like the soot that comes down the chimney.'

And that is how Sooty came to live with Wags. You should see the games they have.

Belinda's Birthday House

BELINDA WAS GOING to have a birthday. It would be in two weeks' time and Billy-Bob knew exactly what he was going to give her. He was going to give her a dolls' house!

That seems rather a big thing – but Billy-Bob was going to make the house himself and then he was going to buy the furniture from the toy shop with the money he had saved up.

Daddy had given Billy-Bob a set of tools at Christmas time so Billy-Bob felt sure he could make a house quite easily. The only thing was he must make it without Belinda seeing him. He explained about it to Mother and she nodded her head.

'Very well, Billy-Bob,' she said. 'You shall make it in the shed outside, and I will keep Belinda here with me so that she won't guess your secret. She will love a birthday house!'

Billy-Bob went out to the shed feeling very important indeed. His tools were there, and he knew there was some wood there too, for he had seen it. He meant to make a wonderful house with four rooms, a big chimney, a front door, and then he would fill it with furniture – beds, chairs, tables, carpets – oh, what fun he was going to have doing his secret for Belinda's birthday!

Billy-Bob set to work – but he wasn't very used to hammering and nailing and sawing. First he hit his thumb and then he sawed a bit off his finger. He sucked it and felt worried. Making a house was more difficult than he had thought.

'Never mind!' said Billy-Bob to himself. 'I must go on trying.'

Just as he was sawing nicely through a big piece of wood to make the back of the house, George the gardener put his head in at the shed.

'Is that you in there, Billy-Bob?' he said. 'Come and help me with something, there's a good boy! I've got to cut down some branches of a tree, and I can't do them properly unless some-one holds them for me. Will you come and help?'

'Well, I'm very busy,' said Billy-Bob. 'I'm just in the middle of something.'

'Oh,' said the gardener. 'What a pity! I don't know how I can do this job out here by myself.'

'Well,' said Billy-Bob, putting down his saw, 'I'll come and help. Wait a minute whilst I put my tools away in the box.'

Billy-Bob helped George the gardener very well indeed – so well that George was able to cut down all the branches very quickly. He *was* pleased.

'That's good!' he said to Billy-Bob. 'I don't know what I should have done without you, Billy-Bob. I suppose there isn't anything I can do for you in return? I'm just going to eat a bit of bread and cheese in the shed, so I'll have a look at what you are doing, if you like.'

Billy-Bob showed George what he was trying to make, and explained to him all about the dolls' house he was going to give Belinda. George ate his bread and cheese and listened.

'Why don't you get a nice-sized box and make that do for the house?' he said to Billy-Bob. 'Then you needn't bother about making the sides and the back or anything. It's there ready for you! Look – here's a good box. I'll turn it on its side – now you've got the roof and the walls and the floor – and you don't want a front part because you can't put the furniture in very well if there's a wall there.'

'Ooh, that's fine!' said Billy-Bob, pleased. 'I'd only just have to paint that, wouldn't I, and make a chimney for the top?'

'Yes,' said George. 'Look here, Billy-Bob, you

gave me a hand just now – let me give *you* a hand at making this house. We could do it together after I've finished my work!'

'Oh, that would be very kind of you,' said Billy-Bob, quite red with delight.

'I've paint and everything here,' said George. 'My, we could make a fine dolls' house between us! I'll help you now if you like. My work is done for the day.'

Well, they began. George made a fine round wooden chimney and Billy-Bob stuck it in the middle of the roof with glue. Then he painted it red! It looked lovely! Then he painted the roof red too, for tiles, and he painted the outside walls a cream colour just like the walls of his own house. George was very clever – do you know what he did? He painted a window with curtains on each side of the house! Billy-Bob thought it looked very real.

'Oooh, I do like it!' he said. 'Won't Belinda be pleased! Can we work again tomorrow, George?'

'Yes,' said the gardener. 'You've been a help to me, and I'll be a help to you. That's the way the world goes round, Billy-Bob!'

Billy-Bob couldn't see the world going round, but he felt as if George was quite right. And the next day the two of them were at work on the house again. What do you suppose they did to the inside of the box? They put a shelf in the middle, so that there was one room upstairs and one room down – and then George thought it would be a good idea to put wallpaper on the walls!

So he and Billy-Bob hunted around and found some old bits of wallpaper and they pasted them carefully all round the box. There was a blue wallpaper for the bedroom upstairs and a red one for downstairs.

'Good!' said George. 'Now we've done the outside of the house, roof, chimney, walls and windows – and the walls inside we've wallpapered. Now you've only got to buy the furniture, Billy-Bob.'

'I'll do that tomorrow,' said Billy-Bob happily. So he emptied his money box the next morning and he and Wags set off to buy the furniture.

But what a great disappointment he had! The dolls' house furniture was dreadfully dear! It cost a great deal of money and poor Billy-Bob hadn't even enough to buy a set of tables and chairs!

'Haven't you anything cheaper at all?' he asked the shop girl. 'I have a lovely empty dolls' house for my sister Belinda, and I *must* have furniture for it.'

'I'm sorry,' said the shop girl, 'but this is all I have.'

Billy-Bob went home, upset and miserable. Mother was out so he couldn't tell her. And, of course, he couldn't tell Belinda anything about it, because it was for her birthday.

'What a long face, Billy-Bob!' said Jane the maid. 'You're as bad as George the gardener to-day. He's got a long face too – as long as yours!'

'Then he must be feeling bad too,' said Billy-Bob. 'What's the matter with him?'

'His mother's got a bad knee so she can't go out and work,' said Jane. 'George is very sorry.'

Billy-Bob was sorry too. He knew George's mother. She was the nicest old lady you can imagine and she went out to do people's washing. She knew lovely stories and could make Billy-Bob and Belinda laugh till they cried.

'I suppose she won't get any money if she can't go out to work?' he said to Jane.

'No, she won't,' said Jane. Billy-Bob thought about the money in his purse. He couldn't buy any furniture for Belinda. He would have to give her the house without furniture. So he could give the money he had saved to George, for his mother.

He ran out to George. 'George!' he called. 'I'm

very sorry about your mother. I do like her so. I couldn't buy any furniture for Belinda's birthday house, so you can have my money to give to your mother. It might last her till her knee is all right again. There is nearly a shilling there.'

George looked down at Billy-Bob and smiled a funny sort of smile. 'You're a good friend, Billy-Bob,' he said, 'and I'll tell my mother what you said. But I've got enough money myself to help her, so she won't need yours. Thank you very much all the same.'

'Oh, I'm glad you've got some money,' said Billy-Bob. 'I didn't think of that. George, isn't a pity I can't buy any furniture? It costs such a lot of money. But never mind, perhaps Belinda will like the house even without furniture.'

Next day George came to work again and he called Billy-Bob. 'My mother said thank you very much for your offer to help her,' he said. 'Her knee is much better – and what do you think, Billy-Bob?'

'What?' said Billy-Bob, in surprise, for George's face was all over smiles.

'Why, my mother says that if you go along to tea with her today, she will show you how to *make* dolls' house furniture out of conkers and pins!'

said George. 'What do you think of that?'

'Out of conkers and pins!' said Billy-Bob, astonished. 'How funny! I've got plenty of conkers.'

'And my mother's got plenty of pins,' said George. 'You go and ask your mother and see what she says.'

Well, Mother said yes, Billy-Bob could go. So that afternoon he said goodbye to Belinda and Wags and set off to the village carrying his bag of conkers. George's mother opened the door to him. Her kitchen smelt so nice. First they had tea – bread and butter and plum jam and currant cake – and then George's mother cleared away and got out a box of pins and a ball of wool.

'Now, Billy-Bob,' she said, 'I'll show you how *I* made furniture for my own dolls' house when I was little! Where are your conkers? I want a nice big one with a flat side, please.'

Billy-Bob gave her one and then watched to see what Mrs George was doing. She took a big pin and stuck it in one side of the conker. She took another and stuck that in opposite. Then a third – and then a fourth – and there was the conker with four legs! The flat part was the top – and the old lady took some more pins and put them in a row to make the back of the chair!

'Oh, it's a most beautiful chair!' said Billy-Bob. 'The conker is the seat – four pins are legs – and six pins make the back of the chair!'

'That's right,' said Mrs George. 'Now see what I do with this wool.' She broke off a long piece and then began to wind it in and out of the pins that made the back of the chair! 'This makes the back strong and pretty,' she said. Billy-Bob watched in delight.

'I'll make one now,' he said. 'It's quite easy!' And soon he was busy making chairs of conkers and pins and wool too. Mrs George made a sofa and a bed and a table and a stool. My goodness, you should have seen all the furniture they made! It didn't take long, and soon there was quite enough for the two rooms in the dolls' house.

Billy-Bob hugged Mrs George when he said goodbye. 'It was kind of you to help me,' he said. 'I didn't think I would get any furniture at all.'

'You deserve a bit of help,' said Mrs George. 'My, won't Belinda be pleased! Look! Here are some pretty bits of stuff to make carpets for the floors. Take those along too.'

Billy-Bob was so happy next day putting in the carpets and the conker furniture. You can't imagine how exciting the dolls' house looked with everything in! Billy-Bob played with it quite a long time himself, arranging everything neatly, and pulling the carpets quite straight.

At last Belinda's birthday came – and when she saw the dolls' house on a chair by the breakfast table Belinda rushed at it with loud squeals.

'Oh! Oh! A birthday house! A dolls' house! Oh, look at the chimney! Oh, look at the furniture! It's even got carpets! Who gave me this?'

'I made it for you, Belinda,' said Billy-Bob, his eyes shining as brightly as Belinda's, because it is such a lovely feeling to give people things you have made. 'I did most of it, but George and Mrs George helped me. Do you like the furniture? It is made of conkers and pins.'

'It is the nicest dolls' house I have ever seen, Billy-Bob,' said Belinda. 'It is my favourite present. I like it best of all. Mother, do you mind me liking Billy-Bob's present better than your lovely book?'

'Of course not,' said Mother. 'I like Billy-Bob's present best too. I know how hard he worked at it.'

Belinda still has the dolls' house – and if any furniture wears out, Billy-Bob just makes some more! Isn't it a good idea!

BELINDA'S BIRTHDAY HOUSE

Also available in the Rewards Series

TALES OF BETSY-MAY

You will love these twenty delightful tales of a small girl, Betsy-May. She is naughty, lovable, kind, awkward, unexpected — like a lot of children and has lots of amusing adventures.

FIVE MINUTE TALES

Here are some of Enid Blyton's favourite stories with lots of her favourite characters too. Follow the adventures of Brer Rabbit, Brer Wolf and many others by reading this delightful collection of stories.

TEN MINUTE TALES

In this collection of ten minute tales we meet Mr Pipkin and his enchanted hat, the dog whose tail wouldn't wag, and many many more. An enchanting collection of stories.

FIFTEEN MINUTE TALES

In this enchanting and exciting book we meet Grumps the Goblin with his horrid pop-out stick, the Cockyolly Bird, the donkey that ran away, Chinky the pixie and many other original and delightful stories.

TWENTY MINUTE TALES

Here are wonderful stories for all of us who like our adventures to last twenty minutes and no more! Open the pages and you will meet the Three Strange Keys, the Goblin Chair and many more amazing adventures to delight you.

THE BLUE STORY BOOK

Here is a collection of amusing and entertaining stories for children, told with all the freshness and humour for which Enid Blyton is so well known.

We have the Very Strange Secret, Tiddley Pom's Pencil, the Whistling Pig, and many others, all told in the simple, straightforward way that children love.

THE RED STORY BOOK

This is the second 'Colour' book in the series. Here are stories of all the things a child knows and loves – its toys, its pets, its home and parents, brothers and sisters. The stories are simply told, and full of interest and humour that will grip the mind of a young child from beginning to end.

THE GREEN STORY BOOK

This is the third 'Colour' book in the series. There are stories of all kinds in it, just the sort a young child loves and understands, told with all Enid Blyton's ingenuity and humour. The Bed That Ran Away, The Tooth Under the Pillow, The Enchanted Wheelbarrow and many many more are here to make children beg for 'just one more' at bedtime.

THE YELLOW STORY BOOK

This is the fourth of Enid Blyton's popular
'Colour' books. With its wealth of stories, each
written in the inimitable Enid Blyton style
combining humour and excitement on every
page.